MORTAL REMAINS

SALLY RIGBY

Storm

Ebook ISBN: 978-1-80508-580-5
Paperback ISBN: 978-1-80508-581-2

Previously published in 2020 by Top Drawer Press.

Cover design: Stuart Bache Design
Cover images: Shutterstock

Published by Storm Publishing.
For further information, visit:
www.stormpublishing.co

ALSO BY SALLY RIGBY

Hidden From Sight

Fear the Truth

ONE

Monday, 14 September

Detective Chief Inspector Whitney Walker glanced around the large oak table where she was seated with all the other senior officers from the Lenchester police force. Her insides clenched. If she could magic herself away to anywhere else, she'd leap at the chance. She didn't want to think about what was about to happen.

Their regular monthly meeting had only one item on the agenda. To finalise details regarding their merger with another force. The Police Federation had been involved and all those present were tasked with informing their teams that they had to reapply for their positions, as there wasn't enough room for everyone. It wouldn't have been so bad if she was going to have an input into which members of her team were going to keep their jobs but, apart from giving them all a reference, the decisions were being made by someone else.

It wasn't just her team who had to fight for their jobs. The idea behind the merger was to make the forces more streamlined and cost-effective, and this meant that she was in the firing line, too. There were more DCIs between the two forces than was required.

The chief constable, Sandra Littleton, was surrounded by five of the most senior officers, including Whitney's immediate superior, Detective Superintendent Tom Jamieson.

Whitney was seated next to Masters, one of the other DCIs.

'It could be me or you, kid,' Masters said, nudging her.

'What?' she replied, bristling at him calling her *kid*. He was in his fifties and had been a DCI for ten years. He might have served for longer than she had, but that didn't mean he was better at his job than she was. Currently, they both had their own teams and were allocated cases depending on workload. Though it did seem that her team picked up most of the murders taking place in the area.

'There are too many DCIs. Some will have to go.'

'That doesn't mean it will be us. They might all go from Willsden,' she said, referring to the force they were merging with.

'Do me a favour,' he said, rolling his eyes. 'They're not going to get rid of all of them. The federation would create merry hell. It will have to be seen as equitable.'

It didn't seem so clear-cut to her. It would be based on merit.

'I'm not making any assumptions.'

'That's your decision, but I'd start dusting off your CV if I were you.' He smirked and she had to sit on her hands not to slap it off his face.

'May I have your attention,' Littleton said.

Pleased that the *discussion* with Masters had come to an end, Whitney focused on what their boss had to say. Like Whitney, she too had come up through the ranks, only much quicker as she was only a couple of years older. Littleton was an excellent leader, unflappable and strong, but also empathic.

Everybody was quiet and looked in the chief constable's

direction. Many years ago, Whitney had aspired to reach that position, but that changed once she'd been promoted to inspector and had realised that the higher up in the force a person got, the less *real* policing was involved. Staying as a DCI gave her sufficient autonomy and kept her involved in solving cases.

'Before we start with the official business, I have an exciting announcement regarding the new station,' Littleton said, cutting into her thoughts. 'We've heard from the construction company that it's now ready for occupation. We'll begin the move in six weeks' time.'

Whitney's heart sank. She loved where they were currently situated. The old Victorian building was close to the city centre which meant she could always pop out to a café and grab herself a coffee whenever she fancied. It also held many memories. She'd been there ever since beginning her training when she was eighteen and a naïve and idealistic recruit. She didn't doubt that the new purpose-built station would be amazing, with all the latest technology and equipment. It was modern and they wouldn't freeze in the winter, as they did at the moment, but it was characterless.

Judging by the sound of excited chatter going on around her, she was the only person with reservations about the move.

'Now for details regarding the impending restructure,' Littleton continued. Putting paid to all the animated discussion. No position was safe, and everyone was concerned about their future. 'We have the Police Federation on board, following negotiations, and we will now begin the selection process. Those of you in the room will have your interviews over the next two to three weeks. Once they're completed, the remaining selections will filter down the ranks. Now we've ironed out the finer details, I would like you all to inform your teams of what will be taking place. HR will email you with the proposed timescales. Although there will be some redundancies, we sincerely hope that these will comprise natural wastage, with people retiring or moving on. Questions?' She scanned the room.

'How much notice will those not successful at retaining their positions be given?' a chief inspector sitting across the table from Whitney asked.

'We'll be talking to the federation about what's going to happen in that respect, but we'd like to ensure the process runs as quickly and as smoothly as possible. The aim is for us to move into the new building with the new teams in place. We don't wish people to make the transition and then lose their positions. It would be unsettling for those who will no longer be working for the force, *and* those who are staying.'

It sounded fine in theory, but theory and practice were two different things.

After fielding several questions, the chief constable ended the meeting and Whitney left the room, dreading how she was going to explain the process to the team.

She pushed open the door to the incident room and as she walked in, she scanned the area. Everyone was working hard at their desks. Now, she was going to have to tell them their jobs could be at risk. She would be there for them if they needed support and knew they would be there for each other.

She'd had enough time to get to grips with what was about to happen, but she'd also put it to the back of her mind as she didn't want the team to realise there was something wrong. The team knew her well enough to recognise when there were issues. She'd followed the compartmentalising ethos of Dr Georgina Cavendish, the forensic psychologist she'd worked with on many cases. It hadn't been easy because that wasn't her usual way of operating, but in this instance, she'd managed to do it.

'Attention, everyone,' she called out, in her usual manner, as she got to the centre of the room. She sucked in a breath. 'I have an important announcement to make and I want one hundred per cent focus from all of you.' She waited while, one by one, her team stopped what they were doing and gave their full attention.

'You're looking worried, guv. Surely, it can't be that bad,' Frank, one of the older members of her team, said. He was a prime candidate for early retirement, if he was offered, as he only had a couple more years to go in the force. Whether he was ready to make that transition now was a different matter. She suspected not. As much as he moaned, and could be lazy, his job was important to him, more for social reasons than financial.

'There are two things I have to tell you,' she said, ignoring Frank's comments. 'First, the new building is ready for us to move into and that will be happening soon. In six weeks, if everything goes to plan.'

'About time, too,' Frank said. 'It's taken them long enough. I, for one, am looking forward to being warm over the winter. I'm fed up with getting chilblains on my hands and feet every year.'

'You need to get yourself some woolly granddad mittens and socks,' Doug said.

'I'm not that old,' Frank said, glaring at him.

'That's a matter of opinion,' Doug quipped.

The spats between the two detective constables were legendary in the department, and most of the time enjoyable to watch. Not today. She needed to keep them focused.

'The next piece of news is that the merger with Willsden is definitely taking place.'

They knew there had been discussions about it, but not how final it was as it had all been kept quiet. Although the team all belonged to the federation, none of them were active, and wouldn't have found out that way.

'I don't see how it can work,' Matt, her detective sergeant, said. 'The new building won't be big enough to house everyone from both forces.' She wasn't surprised he'd come to that conclusion almost immediately.

'This is the bit I'm not happy about. With the merger now confirmed, some jobs are going to disappear. We won't need to double up on every post. I'm sorry to be the one bearing this news, but you're all going to have to reapply for your positions.'

'So, we might lose our jobs?' Frank said, panic etched across his face. She'd been right in her assumption about him. 'What did the Police Federation say? Surely they can't be accepting it without a fight.'

'They've been involved in the negotiations. It is hoped that early retirement, voluntary redundancies, and transfers to other forces will take up most of the slack.'

The air could be cut with a knife.

'So, no mention of striking, then?' Frank asked.

'Not as far as I'm aware. The negotiations have been taking place for a while and were conducted without conflict.'

'What about you, guv?' Doug asked.

'I'll be applying for my position sooner than you. Within the next two or three weeks, I believe.'

'You're a dead cert,' Doug said.

If only she could be sure of that, because right now it was anything but certain. Especially after what Masters had said. She knew she shouldn't let it get to her, but she wouldn't be human if she didn't.

'We can't bank on anything, Doug. I'm in my office if any of you wish to discuss it further in private.'

Was she being a coward for leaving them to it? No. It was a lot for them to take in, and they didn't need their superior officer around while they were discussing it. They needed to feel free to speak openly about it.

'Will you be the one interviewing us?' Frank asked, a hopeful expression in his eyes.

She turned to face him. 'I wish it could be me. But, no.

We've been informed you'll be interviewed by a specialist panel put together by HR.'

'That's ridiculous. Surely, you're the one who knows us best,' Frank said.

She couldn't agree more, and there wasn't one of them she wouldn't fight hard to keep. They were the perfect team. They were loyal, hardworking, and looked out for each other. She couldn't have wished for a better set of people to work with.

'I'll be providing a reference for everyone, but because no one's position is safe, the chief constable thought it best for the interview panels to consist of objective people. I can see the logic behind it.'

She pulled herself up short. Logic. That was George's territory. She'd probably believe what was happening was the most appropriate outcome of the merger plans.

'You've got no worries. There's no one else in Lenchester as good as you,' Frank said.

'I'll second that,' Doug said.

Warmth flooded through her. She didn't need to be told how lucky she was to have them on her side.

'Thanks, guys. But let's not jinx anything. Remember what I said. If you want to speak to me, you know where I am.'

She headed in the direction of her office, which was just off the main incident room.

'Guv,' Matt called out.

She stopped and turned. 'Yes.'

'There was a fire last night at a house in Stanton Road. I've just had a call from the Chief Fire Officer as their initial findings are that it's arson. They want someone out there. Do you want to go, or shall I?'

'Did he tell you anything else? Any injuries or bodies?'

'He didn't say.'

'We'll go together to take a look,' she said, grateful for something to focus on other than the merger.

They took her car and when they arrived at the scene of the crime, an old Victorian terraced house in a student area of town, there was a cordon across what remained of the front gate, preventing anyone from walking down the path and also to block off houses either side. Windows had blown out and glass covered the pavement.

Tall trees lined the road, and the autumn leaves were beginning to change colour. Whitney shivered as a cool blast of wind whistled past them. She pulled her jacket tightly around her.

Although the fire had been put out, the putrid smell lingered. She covered her face with her hand as they walked up to the cordon. One of the fire officers headed towards them.

'Detective Chief Inspector Walker,' she said, flashing her warrant card. 'We were asked to come out.'

'I'm Charlie Fox, crew manager. I was here last night, in command of the incident. One of the neighbours called it in just after midnight. After we controlled the fire and gained access, we found two bodies, one male and one female, in the bedroom overlooking the rear. Cause of death was most likely smoke inhalation, but the pathologist will need to confirm that. An accelerant-soaked cloth had been pushed through the letter box and with all the doors and windows locked, even if the smoke hadn't got to the victims, they wouldn't have been able to get out due to the fire and heat. We believe the victims were students, and two laptops and phones have been taken away by SOCO. The neighbour mentioned that they wouldn't normally be around until next week when term starts.'

Two deaths. Arson.

Murder or manslaughter?

What bastard would do something like that?

'Thanks,' she said appreciating being given all the facts at once, without having to ask for every detail as was so often the case when dealing with a new constable or police community support officer. 'Were the bodies recognisable?'

'Yes. The smoke had reached their bedroom, not the flames. I'll forward you photos that were taken to help with the enquiry.'

'Thanks. Where does the neighbour live? We need to identify the victims straightaway, so their families can be informed. They might be able to help.'

'She's at 119, over there,' he replied, pointing to the left and a few houses down.

'We'll call over shortly. May we go inside?' She wanted to get a sense of the destruction caused by the fire.

'Yes. The building's safe now. Follow me.' Charlie beckoned them in.

The walls had been reduced to charcoal and the toxic stench of burnt plastic hung in the air. Whitney covered her nose. Going into the building wasn't a good idea.

'I can't believe someone would do this,' she said to Matt. 'Did the arsonist think the place was empty? Why were the students here before the start of term? Who owns the house?'

Matt shook his head. 'Beats me, guv.'

'Thanks, Charlie,' she said before turning to Matt and heading back out. 'Let's speak to the woman over the road.'

They marched over to 119 and as Whitney opened the gate to walk down the path, the net curtains twitched. Before they'd reached the front door, it was opened by an elderly woman wearing a pink candlewick dressing gown, tied tightly around her middle.

'I'm Detective Chief Inspector Walker and this is Detective Sergeant Price,' Whitney said holding out her warrant card.

'I'm Mrs Stephenson. I saw you talking to the fireman.'

'I understand you called in the fire last night.'

'Yes. I couldn't sleep and went downstairs for some hot milk and heard a bang. I looked out of the front room window and the house over the road was all lit up. As soon as I realised it was a fire, I phoned 999. What happened to the youngsters inside? Were they taken away in the ambulance?'

Whitney exchanged a glance with Matt. Standing on the doorstep informing someone about a death wasn't advisable, so she decided not to say anything. 'We're waiting to find out. Before the fire, did you look outside and notice anyone or anything out of the ordinary?'

'No, I'm sorry, I didn't.'

'Do you know the couple who lived at the house?'

'I don't know their names, but they would always say hello if I saw them. They were students. I recognised them from last year. I was surprised to see them here as term hasn't started yet. It's very quiet over the summer and I actually prefer it when they're all here.'

'Doesn't the noise bother you?' Matt asked.

'No, I like it. It means I don't get so lonely.'

'Thank you for your help, Mrs Stephenson. You go inside now as it's chilly out here.'

The old woman closed her door and Whitney turned to Matt. 'Let's go back to the station. We need to identify our victims as soon as possible.'

TWO

Monday, 14 September

'Do you have any questions for me?' Whitney asked Matt as she drove them back to the station.

'About the changes?'

'Yes. I'm not promising to know the answer, but if I do, I'll tell you.'

She hoped he realised that he could speak to her in confidence about the situation, and that it would go no further.

'How long have you known?'

She tossed a glance in his direction and witnessed the uncertainty in his eyes. Out of all the team, she imagined he would do well in the interview. Although it would have been better if he'd taken his inspector's exams, as she'd wanted him to, but personal circumstances meant he was happy to stay in his current position.

'I've known for several weeks, but—'

'Why didn't you tell me? I'm your sergeant.'

His tone took her by surprise. Matt was known for keeping his cool, was there something else going on here?

'I'm sorry. You know I wouldn't have kept it from you if I didn't have to. We were instructed to keep it quiet. If they knew I'd leaked the information … well, I don't need to tell you how that would have looked. Had you been in the same position, you wouldn't have told anyone either, would you?'

He stared ahead, out of the car window. 'You're right. I wouldn't have mentioned it,' he finally said.

'Exactly. Are you okay? How's Leigh?' He was being reserved, even for him.

'I'm fine. We had a bit of a scare the other night when Leigh had a bleed. She had to go to the hospital for tests, but she's home now and on bed rest.'

Matt and his wife were expecting their first baby. They'd had IVF and were successful at their first attempt. Leigh was now six months pregnant and it was why he had no desire to go any higher than sergeant, despite being more than capable of passing the inspector exams. Although they were both going to continue working, they'd decided that, because of the time commitment involved, Leigh would pursue her nursing career to a higher level and Matt would remain where he was.

'Why didn't you tell me? You could have had some time off to be with her.'

'You know I don't like to bring my personal life into work.'

'This is different. It's not like you just felt like taking some time off. After we get back, you're to go straight home and spend the rest of the day with Leigh. She'll be grateful to have you there. It must be boring as hell for her having to stay in bed all day.'

'Are you sure?'

'Yes. No arguments. If anything urgent crops up, I'll let you know.'

'Thanks. Her mum has been to see her, which has helped, but it's not the same.'

The rest of the journey took place in silence. When they

arrived back, they headed to the incident room, stopping on the way for Whitney to get a coffee. She was in desperate need of a caffeine fix as it had been hours since her last one and already the day had been extremely taxing.

'Attention, everyone,' she said, clutching at her coffee cup. 'We've just come back from the fire at 122 Stanton Road. We have two bodies, and the fire service has classified it as arson. It's now a crime scene. According to the elderly neighbour who called in the fire, it's a student house. She had seen the two victims arrive a couple of days ago. Although she recognised them, she doesn't know their names. Top priority is to identify them. Fortunately, the bodies weren't badly burnt, so we don't have to wait for DNA testing or dental records. I'll forward photos of them. Ellie, I want you to find out who owns the property as that should help.'

'Yes, guv,' Ellie, the department research guru, said.

Whitney glanced at the officer. There were red rings around her eyes. Had she been crying? Was it over the restructure? Whitney wouldn't be surprised. Ellie was the best researcher she'd ever known, and she'd fought hard to keep her permanently on the team following her secondment to them. Ellie was shy and didn't like change. She'd formed a firm alliance with Matt especially, but the rest of the team looked out for her, too. Whitney would be surprised if Ellie didn't keep her job, but whether she remained on the team was anybody's guess. And that was assuming Whitney kept her job, too. She'd take Ellie to one side later and have a chat, especially now that Matt wasn't going to be there for the rest of the day.

'Phones and laptops have been sent to digital forensics. It's a shame we didn't get to see them first, as Ellie could've used the self-service kiosk to find their identities. Doug, get in touch with Mac and see if they've got anything yet. I hope they weren't too damaged by the smoke or fire.'

'Yes, guv,' he said.

'Frank, check for CCTV cameras close by. I doubt there are any in the actual street, but you might see something of interest on the main roads leading there.'

'Yes guv,' the older officer replied.

'I'm going to let Jamieson know what's happened. I'll be back shortly.'

She left the incident room and braced herself. Her boss never liked hearing there was another death for them to investigate, and she never liked dealing with the fallout from telling him. Ever since he'd arrived at Lenchester, they'd rubbed each other up the wrong way. He'd been fast-tracked into the force without any experience, and it showed. He was more concerned with metrics and accountability than actual police work. It wasn't that she flouted the rules but beginning her career as a constable meant she had a far better idea of how to do the job than those who had bypassed working from the bottom up.

She reached the corridor where his office was, and it was unusually silent. Most of the time his voice could be heard bellowing down the phone, which seemed to be glued to his ear. His door was closed. Again, this was unusual. Maybe he was out. She decided to knock anyway, just in case. He couldn't then accuse her of not keeping him informed.

She tapped on the door and waited.

'Come in,' he called.

She entered his office and did a double take. He was seated behind his desk, staring into space and not shuffling papers as he usually did when anyone came in to see him. She'd always believed it to be an act to convince people he was busy.

'Sir,' she said.

He finally turned to her, tight lines around his eyes. Was there anything wrong? Should she ask? If she did, he'd most likely tell her to mind her own business.

'What do you want, Walker?'

'I've come to inform you that we have two suspicious deaths on our hands.'

'Two? What is it this time?' He let out an exasperated sigh.

He was echoing her thoughts exactly. Just once it would be nice if killers could choose a different location to commit their crimes.

'There's been a fire at a student house in Stanton Road. I've been to the scene and the house has been gutted. The preliminary investigation from the fire service indicates that it's arson. There were two bodies inside, and at this point in time we have no idea whether it's manslaughter or murder.'

'Do we know anything else?'

'Not yet. We haven't identified the victims and are waiting to hear from digital forensics, who we believe have their phones and laptops, so hopefully they will help in this regard.'

'Okay, just get on with it.'

'Is everything all right, sir?' She couldn't stop herself from asking. She'd never seen him so deflated before. When he'd missed out on a promotion six months ago, he became more antagonistic, rather than appearing so down.

'Sit down,' he said.

Her jaw dropped. That had to be a first. She did as he'd requested.

'Yes, sir.'

'Got any thoughts about your future here?'

None that she wanted to share with him. He could be on her interview panel, and she didn't want to inadvertently provide him with any ammunition.

'Not really. I don't want to have to apply for my position, but I have no choice. More importantly, I'm not happy about having no say in the interviews of my team. I'm the one who knows them and their capabilities best.'

That was the first time she'd actually articulated her feelings and, even though it was to Jamieson, she felt better knowing she had someone who understood. At least, she hoped he did.

'You might be interested to know that I, too, am having to reapply for my job. I've only just been informed. I didn't expect that to happen.'

Did knowing that he was going through exactly the same as she was make her feel better? Not really.

'Why not?'

'I understand your level and lower having to. It makes sense within the restructuring framework. Even though Willsden has a detective superintendent, Lenchester is a much larger force and so the role should be mine, without any of this nonsense. Don't you agree?'

Interesting. They all were feeling the same. She'd bet George would have some psychological slant on that. As for him asking her opinion, she was sure he didn't really want it, and instead expected her to agree with him.

'What about the chief constable?' She figured that was a better question to ask, rather than answering his.

'She remains in her position. Hardly surprising, as she was the one who orchestrated the whole thing.'

'Yes, that does make sense. I'm sure your position is secure, sir.'

'Maybe. But it's not a situation I wish to be in. I'd be lying if I said I wasn't concerned.' His face was drawn.

Considering he'd applied for a promotion recently she'd have thought this to be an ideal time to carry on his search for a new position. Then again, it would look better for him if he was actually employed when he applied.

'It shouldn't be an issue. We're the larger and more high-profile force, so surely at the higher levels there won't be much change.'

She said that more to pacify him, as she had no real basis on which to make the claim.

'But ... it doesn't matter. Carry on with your work. You don't need to bother yourself with issues concerning me.'

'Okay, sir. If you do want to talk any time, I'm here.'

Like that was going to happen. Now he was in a relationship with Caroline, the family liaison officer, he had someone to go to when he needed. Assuming that he was still involved with her. Another topic she had no intention of broaching.

'Thank you for the offer, but I'll be fine. Your time is better spent concentrating on capturing this arsonist. We certainly don't need unsolved cases on our hands at a time like this. Off you go.' He waved at her with his trademarked flick of the hand and lowered his gaze to the folders on his desk.

She left and went downstairs. To be honest, she was glad he had to reapply for his position the same as the rest of them. It wouldn't have been fair otherwise. Not that it would be a problem for him. She'd have thought he would have been a shoo-in as he appeared to be on the good side of his superiors. He also ran a tight ship, albeit ineffectively at times, in her opinion. Maybe the higher echelons had seen what she had. If that was the case then it would prove she wasn't being unfair when she'd criticised him, even if George believed she was.

Thinking about the forensic psychologist reminded her she would have to get in touch regarding the arson attack. Her opinions were always welcome.

She returned to the office and headed straight for Ellie's desk. 'Found anything yet?'

'I've located the owner of the property. Sidney Drake. He owns a number of student houses in the area.'

'We need to get on to him straightaway. What about the names of our victims?' Whitney asked, as she went over to see Doug.

'I've spoken to Mac and they don't have anything yet, as they've been working on other cases,' Doug said.

'It's been over twelve hours since the fire and still the families don't know. That's not good enough.'

'I'll contact him again,' Doug said.

'No. Ellie can do it. She has an excellent relationship with Mac and manages to get him to do things us lesser mortals can't.'

She headed back to Ellie's desk. 'Do you have details for the landlord?'

'Yes. I'll text them to you.' Ellie turned back to her keyboard and her eyes widened. 'Hang on a minute, guv. This is interesting. It seems that he's behind on his mortgage payments.'

A motive?

'Only for that particular property?'

'No. All ten of them,' Ellie said.

'It looks like we could have a motive. Text me Drake's details and then contact Mac and explain how urgent it is that we identify the victims and ask if he could hurry with the phones and laptops as they're our quickest route to the information. He'll listen to you. After that, continue digging into the landlord and see what else you can come up with. I'm going to contact Dr Cavendish. I'd like her to come in with me to interview him.'

THREE

Monday, 14 September

Forensic psychologist, Dr Georgina Cavendish, was seated at the desk in her office at the university, staring at an email that had landed in her inbox only a few minutes earlier. It was an invitation to an exhibition taking place at an art gallery in Lenchester featuring the work of sculptor Ross Wogan. Her ex-boyfriend.

They'd broken up after he'd proposed, and she'd turned him down. He'd wanted to continue seeing her, but at the time she'd believed it wasn't a good idea. She missed him now, though. Despite trying hard to get on with her life, always at the back of her mind, there were thoughts of him and the good times they'd had together in the past.

She shook her head in an attempt to rid the image of his brow crinkling when he was concentrating. That sort of behaviour wasn't her. She was becoming more like Whitney. Emotional. In the past, she'd never let her feelings get in the way, but since she'd been hanging around with the DCI, she'd gradually changed. She was still nowhere near as emotional as Whitney, but there were definite changes. Whether that was a good thing or not, remained to be seen.

Should she go to the exhibition? It had been in the pipeline when they were together, but the date hadn't been set.

Had Ross asked the gallery to invite her or was it just that she was on their mailing list? She often went to art exhibitions, so it was most likely that.

But what should she do? Ignore the invite or go? She rubbed her brow, hating the indecision plaguing her. She stared once more at the email and was about to close it when her phone rang. Whitney's name flashed up on the screen.

'Hello,' she said, holding the phone to her ear.

'It's Whitney.'

'Yes, I know,' she said, in a clipped tone.

'Is everything okay?' Whitney sounded concerned.

Why was it the officer was always able to identify when there was anything untoward going on? It was uncanny.

'Yes,' she replied, not wanting to discuss her dilemma. 'I'm sitting at work, deciding what task to tackle next. The students haven't yet started, and I'm preparing my lectures. What can I do for you?'

'We've got some suspicious deaths,' Whitney said in the tight voice she only used when things were bad at the station.

Murders put intense pressure on the officer and her team. George admired their resilience.

'Tell me about them,' she said, grateful to be able to put Ross and his blasted invite to the back of her mind.

'There was a fire in a student house, and we have two bodies. The fire service has indicated that it's arson. Whether it's murder or manslaughter, we don't yet know. We haven't yet identified the victims but have found the landlord. He's behind on the mortgage payments for all his properties.'

'That certainly could be a reason to commit arson.'

'We need to investigate him further. Are you able to get out today and come with me to interview him?'

Being with Whitney would be a welcome distraction and she couldn't think of anything she'd rather do. It would do her good to get out and focus on something other than Ross.

'Okay, count me in. I'll come and collect you.'

'Excellent. We can have a catch-up on the way as it seems ages since we last saw each other.'

'I'll be with you in twenty minutes.'

George closed her laptop, grabbed her bag and jacket, and gratefully left the office. Despite what she'd said to Whitney, she was almost up to date with her administration and lecture preparation for the new students.

She had been in touch with Ross since the break-up. He'd contacted her a few months ago when her father was going through problems after being charged with tax evasion. They'd spoken on the phone, but he hadn't asked to meet, and she hadn't suggested it. He'd called to check that she was okay, after having seen all the hype in the media. It was typical Ross behaviour. He'd always been very considerate.

Her father was out on bail and the case not due to come to court until sometime next year. He believed he'd receive a hefty fine and no jail time. She hoped he was correct. It would destroy her parents if he was wrong.

The public had been quick to forget his misdemeanour, as his private practice was now as buoyant as it always had been. He was the go-to cardiac surgeon for the rich and famous. For the moment, everything was as it always had been, apart from he was now paying his taxes.

Her brother had kept her up to date on the situation, as her parents were too busy to contact her. Something she was grateful for as too much time in their company, to quote Whitney, sent her batshit crazy.

When she reached the university staff car park, she got into her Land Rover Discovery. For a long time, she'd been thinking of changing it for a Porsche, but with everything going on with her father and Ross, she'd pushed the decision to the back of her mind. She drove to the station and headed to the incident room.

As usual, the hubbub of everyone working hit her as soon as she walked in. It was a large room and there were twenty desks in pairs facing each other. There were screens on each one. As she walked through, some of the team looked up and acknowledged her with a smile. It was always good to see them. A sense of belonging washed over her. It wasn't something she'd ever encountered at the university, despite the fact it was where she'd spent most of her career.

She scanned the room but couldn't see Whitney, so she headed towards her separate office.

The door was open, and Whitney was seated at her desk with the phone to her ear. She gestured for George to come in and sit down. When she'd finished the call, Whitney beamed.

'It's so good to see you. How's everything going?'

Should she tell Whitney the whole story, or the abridged version? Actually, it wasn't even a question. There was too much going on for George to muddy the waters with her issues. George shrugged and sat down.

'It's always hectic at this time of year. The students will be back soon. It will be good to get back to some normality.'

'I'm sure you're well prepared,' Whitney said, a knowing smile on her lips.

'Yes, I'm ready for them. How's Tiffany?' George asked about Whitney's daughter who was overseas in Australia on a working holiday. She had a soft spot for the young woman, ever since being instrumental in her rescue from some psychotic, murdering twins.

'She's doing well, thanks. She's in touch most days, but I do miss her. I can't wait for her to come back. How's your dad? Any news on the court date?'

'He's out on bail and back working as if nothing has happened. The case is due to be heard next year and I doubt I'll hear any more about it until then. Tell me about the fire.'

'It's arson and we have two victims who are students. Right now, we don't know much more. I'm anxious to identify them as both families need to be informed.'

'Do you suspect the owner of the property?'

'Yes. He owns several houses in the area and is behind on his mortgage payments for all of them. Can you think of a better reason to set fire to your own properties?'

'If he is the culprit, maybe he didn't realise the victims were there. Term hasn't started yet, so he could have thought the house was empty.'

'The neighbour mentioned she was surprised to see them back already. If he believed the house to be empty and he's guilty of setting fire to it, it will be manslaughter and not murder. We'll find out more when we see him. That's why I was keen to have you with me. You'll spot anything suspicious in his body language.'

George enjoyed watching Whitney questioning people, not only to assess whether the interviewee was speaking the truth, but she admired the officer's expertise in interview situations.

'My car?'

'You even have to ask?' Whitney stood up and stacked the folders she'd been working on to one side of her desk.

'Isn't that part of the ritual?' She arched an eyebrow.

'It is, and I'm impressed you realised.' Whitney gave a warm smile.

'I think we've been out together enough times for it to imprint itself on my muscle memory.'

'Once we're away from the station, I'll tell you what's going on here, because there are going to be some major changes,' Whitney said, changing the subject, her smile fading and replaced by a tight line.

'Changes?' George frowned. Would they affect her?

'Yes. Big ones. I'll tell you when we're in the car.'

FOUR

Monday, 14 September

'Wait for me,' Whitney called out, trying and failing to keep up with George's long-legged stride across the car park.

George turned. 'Sorry, I didn't even notice you weren't with me.'

'Because you're preoccupied with something else?' Whitney quirked an eyebrow as she finally reached her friend.

'What made you think that?'

'I'm psychic. Apart from that, I know you well enough now to see behind your usual air of logic and no-nonsense. But I won't press you. I'll wait until you're ready to spill.'

'Thank you.' George flashed a grateful look in her direction.

Whitney had come to know the forensic psychologist very well. It wasn't like that when they'd first met and worked on a case together. Sparks had flown but, since then, after George had helped save Whitney's daughter from being murdered, they now had a bond that was unbreakable.

Despite their occasional falling out, Whitney knew they were there for each other forever.

'Unlike you, I'm willing to share what's going on,' Whitney said once they were seated in the car and before George had even left the car park. 'And there's a lot.'

'I'm all ears,' her friend said, starting the engine and pulling out of the car park into traffic.

'You know, the new purpose-built station?'

'The one you don't want to move into even though it's going to be a much more comfortable and suitable option for all of you? I believe you have mentioned it to me on several occasions,' George replied.

'You do know that sarcasm doesn't become you?' Whitney quipped, rolling her eyes.

'I was simply stating a fact,' George said in a prim voice. 'There was no intention of anything else.'

'If you say so. Anyway, yes. That's the one. The moving date has been set and it's not just us. We're merging with Willsden, another police force. Their force is smaller than ours and is situated thirty miles from here.'

'How's it going to affect you?' George asked.

'Give me a crystal ball and I'll tell you.'

'I don't understand,' George said, frowning. 'Are you saying that you don't know what the outcome will be?'

'That's exactly what I'm saying. I have no idea how it's going to pan out and that's what's so unsettling. In an ideal world it won't make much of a difference, other than I'll have a different office. On the other hand, everything could change beyond recognition.' Whitney massaged the back of her neck and let out a long breath.

'You'll have to be more explicit.'

'We *all* have to reapply for our jobs. From top to bottom, I believe, apart from the chief constable, who has a golden ticket.'

'A *golden ticket*?'

'It's just a saying. It means her job is safe and she doesn't have to reapply for it.'

George tossed a quick glance in her direction. 'Does that mean you could end up out of work?'

Trust her to get straight to the point.

'I'm not sure what's going to happen. Obviously, there are going to be some redundancies because they don't need double the number of officers. Economies of scale, and all that. They're hoping for natural wastage. People moving to a different force or taking early retirement or redundancy.'

'Is redundancy something you'd consider?'

'What do you think? Of course not,' she said, not giving George a chance to answer. 'Being stuck at home all day with nothing to do would drive me batshit crazy. I'm going to apply for my job and see what happens. Maybe I should start doing the lottery. If I win millions, being out of work won't matter.'

'But surely your position isn't in doubt. In my opinion, it would be a foolish move to let go someone of your calibre. Your reputation, together with all the cases you and the team have solved, must stand you in good stead.'

'My *reputation* as someone who rubs up her senior officers the wrong way and won't be swayed from following a course of action if she believes it's going to solve a crime, irrespective of what others might say. Is that what you mean?' Whitney asked, her shoulders slumped.

'I think you're denigrating yourself unnecessarily.'

Was she? George was an expert at seeing through the crap, whereas she tended to get bogged down in her emotions.

'Maybe, but there's not going to be room for everyone at my level and there are some people who think they should take precedence over me. We don't know what the competition's like. The officers from Willsden could be top-notch.' Despondency washed over her. Perhaps she shouldn't have voiced her concerns out loud. It'd only made her feel worse, and they still had a job to do.

'What about the rest of your team, have they been informed?'

'I told them earlier. They have to be interviewed, too. It's a worry as I'm not sure they'll all retain their jobs. Those who don't could apply to other forces, providing they don't mind moving. Fine for the young ones with a career ahead of them. But what about Frank? He's due to retire in a couple of years so it's unlikely he'll be offered a job elsewhere.'

'Do you think he'd like to take early retirement?' George asked.

'I doubt it. He's not ready, if what he's told me in the past is anything to go by. But he might be forced to.' She groaned. 'This whole situation is just unbearable.'

'When are the interviews?'

'Soon. At least, mine is. I'm not yet sure of the date, but definitely within the next couple of weeks.' She glanced out of the window as they turned into Carlton Street. 'Pull in here,' she said as they drew up outside a scruffy office building. 'This is where he's based.'

'It's a bit run down,' George said.

They walked to the entrance of the five-storey building, and Whitney scanned the list of companies in there. '*Drake Holdings*. That's the place,' she said, pressing the intercom buzzer.

'Hello,' a female voice came over the intercom.

'We're here to see Mr Drake,' Whitney said, choosing not to say she was from the police. Giving a warning wasn't advisable if at all possible.

'Come on in. You'll have to walk up as the lift isn't working.'

The door buzzed and they went into the old 1960s office building, which was cold and damp with paint peeling off the walls. By the time they'd reached the fifth floor, they were both out of breath.

'We're so unfit,' Whitney puffed. 'Maybe we should start some sort of exercise regime.'

'I already do yoga and go walking. Perhaps I should take up running, too,' George said.

They headed along the corridor until coming to a door with *Drake Holdings* sign-written on it. The white letters were faded and some of the paint had worn off. Whitney pushed open the door and they walked in. Sitting behind a large desk was an older woman with blonde hair and red lips.

'I'm Detective Chief Inspector Walker, and this is Dr Cavendish. We've come to see Mr Drake.'

The woman's eyes widened. 'I'll let him know you're here. He's in his office.' She pointed to the closed door on the right and stood. Whitney gestured with her hand for her to remain where she was.

'No need. We'll go through ourselves.'

Whitney knocked on the door, and they walked in without waiting for an answer. An imposing, overweight man with a shaved head sat behind the desk, staring at a computer screen.

'Sidney Drake?' Whitney asked.

'Yes,' he said, glancing up.

'I'm Detective Chief Inspector Walker and this is Dr Cavendish.'

'What is it?' His panicked eyes darted from Whitney to George as he stood. He must have been at least six feet three. Whitney had to crane her neck to look at him.

'May we sit?'

'Yes, of course,' he said, as he walked around to the front of his desk and removed the stacks of files from both chairs.

'I understand you own 122 Stanton Road,' Whitney said.

'That's correct. Has there been a break-in?'

'We're here to inform you there was a fire there last night.'

'A fire?' He raised his eyebrows in surprise. 'How much damage was done?'

'It was extensive. Two people were in there at the time, and they both died.'

'Dead. That can't be right. My student houses don't start filling up until next week.'

His eyes registered shock, but was it genuine?

'How does it work when renting to students? Do you just rent for the academic year?' George asked.

'They rent from September first through to June thirtieth. But most don't move in straight away. After the first month's rent and bond has been paid, they can collect their keys. But nobody had collected the one for Stanton Road. Except ...' He paused.

'Yes,' Whitney prompted.

'It's the same group of students who rented it last year. I prefer it that way then at least I know my tenants. They might still have a key.'

'Might? Don't you know?' Whitney asked.

'I'd have to check. They do have to hand keys in when they leave, at the end of their lease. But they could have had an extra one cut.'

'How many students rent this house?'

'I'll have to ask Cynthia.' He picked up his phone and pressed a key. 'How many students in 122 Stanton Road?' He nodded and replaced the handset. 'Four. They are friends but each have a separate rental agreement. Do you know who was in the house?'

'Not yet. We'd like details of all of them. Have you met them in person?' She was debating showing him the photos of the victims, then decided against it as she didn't want it to be public knowledge until the families had been informed.

He lifted the phone again. 'Cynthia, bring in the tenants' details from Stanton Road.'

'What were you doing last night, between eleven and one in the morning?' Whitney asked once he'd replaced the phone.

'I was at home.'

'Can anybody vouch for you?'

'Why are you asking? Surely you don't think I'd want to set fire to my own property?' His hands were balled into tight fists and resting on his desk.

'We understand that you're behind on your mortgage repayments,' Whitney said.

His eyes flickered. 'Who told you that?'

'We do our research.' She locked eyes with him. He surely wasn't naïve enough to think they wouldn't have knowledge of his financial situation.

'I admit I'm in a bit of difficulty, but it's nothing that can't be sorted out. I have an appointment with the bank today.' He dipped his head to the left.

He was definitely hiding something.

'Was the house in Stanton Road insured?' George asked.

'All of my houses are. I'm in business, and the bank demands it.'

'So, if it was burnt down, you'd be able to collect insurance money,' George said.

Whitney glanced at her, grateful that she'd got straight to the point, not allowing Drake any time to pull his thoughts together. If Whitney had been more on the ball, instead of having half a mind on the crap going on at work, she'd have done the same.

'What are you accusing me of?' This time he looked up, eyes narrowed.

'We're trying to ascertain the facts,' Whitney said. 'You haven't answered my question. Can anyone vouch for you being at home during the times I asked?'

'My wife was with me,' he said flatly.

'We'll be contacting her to verify,' Whitney said. 'Let—'

The knock on the door interrupted her. Cynthia walked in holding a manila folder which she handed to Drake. 'These are the details of the tenants in Stanton Road you asked for.'

'Thank you.'

Cynthia glanced from Drake to Whitney and George. 'Is everything okay?'

'There's been a fire at the property and two people have died,' Whitney answered.

Colour drained from her face. 'Oh, my goodness. That's dreadful.' She grabbed hold of the desk. 'Do you know who was in there?' she asked, looking at Whitney.

'Not yet. That's what we're investigating.'

'Cynthia, why don't you make us both a cup of tea while I finish up with the police. We've had a shock,' Drake said, suddenly taking charge.

'Yes. I'll do that. I won't be long.' She ran her hand through her hair and shuddered. 'Such a dreadful business. Nothing like this has happened before.' She turned and left the office.

'Here's the file,' Drake said, handing it to Whitney. 'Is there anything else you want me for?'

'Your wife's phone number.' She passed over her notebook and he wrote it down.

'This is our landline. She's at home most of the time.' He slid the notebook back and Whitney pocketed it.

'We will most likely want to speak with you again,' she said.

'Do I need a solicitor?'

Everyone asked the same question. Damn TV programmes.

'Only if you think you need one,' Whitney said. Next to her, George tilted her head, obviously taking in his reaction.

'I didn't do anything.'

'Thank you for your time. We'll be in touch.'

They left the building, walked down the five flights of stairs, and headed outside. She was grateful to breathe in some fresh air, rather than the damp, musty, stale air from inside the building.

'He was certainly shifty,' Whitney said.

'Agreed. There was something he wasn't telling us,' George said. 'It was evident by his eye movements and his lack of blinking when you asked him his whereabouts. But he did seem genuinely shocked by the deaths. His deceit may have nothing to do with the fire.'

'As we don't know which of the students are our victims, I'm going to contact Ellie and let her have the names of the students living in the house, although hopefully Mac would have found their identities by now. Then we'll visit the families, if they're in the area.'

FIVE

Monday, 14 September

'Mac has come through for us. One of the victims comes from Dorset, and I've arranged for the local police to inform the family. The other family lives in Rugby. We'll go there now, if you're still okay to come with me,' Whitney said to George after she'd ended her call with Ellie.

George was more than happy to spend time with Whitney, as it stopped her from thinking about Ross, and she could concentrate on helping with the case. It cut both ways, too, as it prevented Whitney from thinking too much about her future. It certainly seemed uncertain and nothing was a foregone conclusion. If Whitney left the force, it would change George's work with the police, too. Would she work with another DCI if Whitney wasn't around? She loved working with the police, but part of that was because of the relationship she'd established with Whitney and the team. The thought of starting again wasn't something she wanted to consider.

'Yes, that's fine. I can stay with you for the day,' she said.

Within thirty minutes, they'd arrived outside the modern

detached house in a suburban area of Rugby. There was a red Toyota Corolla in the driveway.

'It looks like someone's in,' Whitney said, as they walked up the path and she rang the bell.

A woman wearing gym gear, her dark hair pulled back with a headband, answered the door. Beads of sweat were on her brow. Had she just returned from doing some exercise?

'Yes?' she said looking at them and frowning.

'I'm Detective Chief Inspector Walker from Lenchester CID, and this is Dr Cavendish. Are you Mrs Smythe?'

'Yes,' her voice had become shrill. 'What is it?'

'We'd like to come in and speak to you regarding your daughter, Cara.'

The colour leeched from her face. 'What's happened?'

'Please may we come in? Are you alone?'

'Yes, my husband's at work. He'll be back soon for lunch.'

Mrs Smythe ushered them into the hall and through to an open-plan lounge, dining, kitchen area.

'Please sit down,' Whitney said gently. Once the woman was seated on the dark blue sofa, she cleared her throat. 'I'm very sorry to inform you that last night there was a fire at 122 Stanton Road, Lenchester, while Cara was inside. Unfortunately, she didn't survive.'

Mrs Smythe stared at Whitney, her eyes glazed. 'Fire?' she repeated.

'Yes. We're sorry for your loss.'

'Are you sure?' She leant forward and let out a groan.

'What time is your husband due home?' George asked.

She stared at George. 'Soon. For lunch.'

George glanced at her watch. It was already twelve-thirty.

'We'll wait with you until he arrives back,' Whitney said.

After a couple of minutes, the door slammed. 'I'm home,' a male voice called out.

'I'll go,' George said, jumping up and heading into the hall.

'Who are you?' he said, the smile on his face disappearing.

'I'm Dr Cavendish. I'm with Detective Chief Inspector Walker. If you'd like to come inside, we've been with your wife.'

'Why? What's happened?'

'Please, come inside, Mr Smythe.'

He followed her in and stood beside the sofa. His wife stared blankly ahead.

'I'm sorry to tell you that there was a fire last night and your daughter, Cara, was inside the building. She didn't survive,' Whitney said.

He dropped down onto the sofa next to his wife and stared at them.

George hated having to watch their grief. She'd been with Whitney enough times to realise that everyone reacted differently to the news. But it never got easier. She admired Whitney's strength in dealing with these situations.

'Are you able to answer a few questions for us?' Whitney asked, after he'd seemed to compose himself.

He nodded. 'Yes.'

'Cara wasn't there on her own. She was with Hamish Ronson. Do you know him?'

'Yes, he was Cara's boyfriend. They've been together for a couple of years now.'

'Unfortunately, he didn't survive either. We're treating the fire as suspicious as the fire officer believes it was arson.'

'Arson? Are you telling us someone deliberately targeted them?'

'We don't know yet if they were specifically targeted.'

'The fire happened last night, yet you're only just telling us now. Why?' he demanded.

'I'm sorry it took longer to inform you than we would have liked. We've only just managed to get the details of your daughter and her partner,' Whitney said.

'I want to see her,' he said.

'We will need a formal identification of Cara, but before that can be arranged, I need to speak to the pathologist as to when it can be done,' Whitney said. 'Would you be able to tell us why they were both in Lenchester so long before the start of the new term?'

'They wanted to have some time alone before their friends arrived. They hadn't seen much of each other over the holidays because Hamish lived in Dorset and Cara was up here.'

'If they'd only stayed home this wouldn't have happened,' Mrs Smythe said. She began shaking, and her husband put his arm around her shoulders.

'I'm sorry we don't have any answers yet, but we will keep you up to date with the investigation. Is there anyone I can ask to be with you?' Whitney said.

'No, we're okay on our own,' Mr Smythe said. 'I'll let the rest of the family know later.'

'When did you last speak to Cara?' Whitney asked.

'On Friday. Hamish collected her and drove them both to Lenchester. She phoned to let us know she'd arrived and that she was settled in,' Mr Smythe said.

'Did she contact you every day?'

'She spoke to her mother more than me.'

'We would text most days. But I know they were busy catching up with each other and going out to have some fun ...' Mrs Smythe leant forward resting her head in her hands.

The grief in the room covered them all like a blanket.

'Did Cara have any enemies that you know of?'

'No. She was a happy girl, and always had lots of friends,' Mr Smythe said.

'What about Hamish? Did Cara ever mention him having any problems?' Whitney asked.

'Not that I know of. Did she say anything to you?' he asked his wife.

'No.' She shook her head.

'Who knew they were going back to Lenchester early?' Whitney asked.

'I'm not sure. I assume they might have told their friends. Cara didn't say,' Mr Smythe said. 'They're only kids. Why would anyone want them dead?'

'We don't know the fire was directed at them. That's what we're investigating at the moment. If you do think of anything that might help with our enquiries, please let me know.' Whitney handed him her card. 'We'll be in touch to organise the identification as soon as possible.'

They let themselves out and returned to the car.

'God, I hate this part of the job.' Whitney leant back in her seat and rubbed her brow. 'We're assuming that they died of smoke inhalation from what we were told by the fire officer. I want to confirm with the pathologist in case other factors were involved. I hope Claire's working this case. We'll call in to see her later.'

SIX

Monday, 14 September

'Do you remember that earlier I said I'd wait until you were ready to tell me what was wrong?' Whitney said, as George turned onto the main road and overtook a lorry.

'Yes. Why?'

'I've changed my mind. I need your full attention on this case and you're not giving it. I've asked you twice whether you've come across many arson attacks in the past and you blanked me both times.'

George sighed. Her friend was right, she'd been thinking about the exhibition and what attending would entail. She'd run through the various scenarios, and none of them were sitting right. She'd deduced that it would be for the best if she pretended the invite hadn't arrived. But was that likely to happen? Whitney was the one with the ostrich mentality on occasions, not her. It was perplexing, to say the least.

'Sorry.'

'Would you like to share now?'

Would she? No, she didn't like sharing anything personal. *Will she?* That was a different question altogether.

'Earlier today I received an email from Lenchester gallery inviting me to an exhibition they're holding of Ross's work.'

'Ah. So that's it. Do you still think about him?' Whitney turned towards her.

She would have thought the answer to that question was obvious. She wouldn't be worrying about the situation if she wasn't.

'I've never stopped,' George admitted, hating the way her chest pounded just from mentioning his name.

'Tell me about the exhibition.'

'It's a solo show.'

Whitney gave a low whistle. 'I might not know much about art, but I'm guessing if it's only featuring him, it's a big deal. I had no idea he was so famous.'

'Yes, it is prestigious. The gallery is well known in art circles. I'm very happy for him, it's well deserved.'

'Why were you sent an invitation?'

'That's what I've been wondering. It could be because I'm on their mailing list, or Ross might have added me to the guest list when it was first planned and forgotten to take me off.'

'Or he could have asked them to invite you. Is that something he'd do?'

'He knows I like art, and especially his work. So, yes, I suppose he could have suggested it.'

Did she want that to be the only reason? Or would she prefer that it was so he could see her again? If she was being honest with herself, it could be the latter.

'Are you going to go?'

'I don't know,' she said, shaking her head.

'Have you been in touch with Ross at all since your relationship finished?'

40

'He texted and phoned when my father was arrested, but other than that, I haven't seen or spoken to him.'

'Let me put it this way, then. Do you *want* to go?' Whitney asked.

The sixty-four thousand dollar question.

'I think so, but I don't want to open up a can of worms.'

'Only you could compare seeing Ross with a worm,' Whitney said, shaking her head.

'It's a perfectly common enough saying. I'll admit, it would be good to see him. We have no obstacles to overcome as we didn't exactly leave on bad terms. Apart from the fact that after I told him I didn't want to get married or live with him, he left without saying goodbye.'

'I'd consider that an obstacle,' Whitney retorted.

'So, you think I shouldn't go?' Deflation washed over her. Why was this so hard?

'I'm not saying that. It's got to be your decision.'

'It would be nice to see him,' she admitted, as much to herself as to her friend.

'Would you like me to come with you?'

That was an option. Whitney was always good company and it would stop Ross from thinking that she'd only gone because of him. Actually, scrap that thought. Ross knew that she was more than happy to visit places alone.

'I'll think about it and let you know. If I do go, then it would be nice to have you accompany me.'

They continued their journey in silence. George was engrossed in her thoughts, while Whitney was on her phone.

* * *

'Attention, everyone,' Whitney said, once they'd arrived back at the incident room. 'George and I visited the landlord and have been to see the family of Cara Smythe. The victims, who were a couple, came back to Lenchester early to spend some time together before the start of the academic year. The landlord had no idea they'd returned. He remains on our radar but he does have an alibi so we need to consider whether the fire was set by someone else. Frank, have you had a look at CCTV footage around the houses?'

'As you suspected, there aren't any close by, guv, because it's a residential area.'

She bit back her frustration. The UK was known for having more CCTV cameras than most countries in the world, keeping track of everyone's movements, yet the one place she needed some they weren't there. Typical.

'Have we received the fire officer's report yet, Doug?'

'No, guv,' he said.

'Do we know whether there have been any other unexplained fires recently?' She doubted there had been, or she would have heard. But she'd learnt never to take anything for granted.

'This is the first,' Ellie confirmed.

'We need to know why it was this house. Were the couple intended victims, or was it unfortunate that they were there at the time? If it's the former, we need to know why they were targeted. Ellie, I want you to look into the couple's friends, social media, families, and all other aspects of their lives. According to Cara Smythe's parents, their daughter didn't have enemies. But that doesn't necessarily mean she didn't. We also need to know more about Hamish. Doug, contact the CID in Dorset and ask them to speak to his parents again. I'm going to see Jamieson to arrange a press conference. A member of the public might have noticed if there was anyone hanging around.'

She left the incident room and went upstairs to see the super. His door was open, so she gave it a tap and walked in.

'Yes, Walker?' he said, looking up from his computer screen.

'We need to arrange a press conference regarding the fire.

I've just come from seeing the owner of the property. The victims were both students. Our priority is to find out if they were deliberately targeted. We also need to discover if anyone was seen hanging around, acting suspiciously. In my experience, arsonists typically like to stay and admire their handiwork.'

She didn't get the fascination with fire that some people had. The way a fire could get out of control so quickly, and its effects be so devastating, scared her.

'Leave it with me. I'm not available this afternoon as I have an appointment. I'll arrange it for tomorrow.'

'First thing in the morning would be best, if that's possible.'

'Yes, that works for me.' He picked up a file from the pile on his desk, a signal he'd terminated their conversation.

As she headed down the corridor, her phone rang. It was Claire, the pathologist. That was a surprise. Usually it was Whitney chasing her up.

'Walker.'

'When are you coming over?' Claire asked, not even bothering to say hello. 'I've examined the bodies from the fire, which I understand has been classified as arson, and I wish to discuss my findings with you.'

'We'd planned to come over to see you shortly. What have you got?'

'I'll tell you when you get here,' Claire said, her tone clipped.

She should have known better than to ask the pathologist. She preferred their interaction to be on her terms. The only reason Whitney went along with it was because Claire was the best pathologist they had. In fact, she'd put money on her being the best in the country.

'Okay. I'll grab George and we'll see you soon.'

When she arrived back at the incident room, George was sitting at a desk staring at one of the computer screens. She headed over. The screen contained what appeared to be an academic article. Was she doing some of her own work?

'Claire phoned me. She wants to see us, which fits in with our plans. Are you okay to leave now, or are you working on something?' She nodded at the screen.

'I'm refreshing my knowledge. This is a paper on the psychological traits of serial arsonists. It's very informative, if we need it.'

'And here we go again with the—'

'Don't even think of saying the word,' George said, glaring at her.

Jinxing, jinxing, jinxing.

'Let's go then,' she said.

George took her bag from the back of the chair and slung it over her shoulder.

When they arrived at the morgue they went in through the double doors and, as usual, Whitney was hit by the *morgue stench* as she thought of it. An intense chemical smell from strong cleansers and preservatives. It didn't matter how many times she was there, it always got to her.

It beat her how Claire and the other morgue staff managed to put up with it. When they arrived at the lab, Claire was sitting in the small office situated to the side of the main lab area. She was staring into space, her eyes glazed.

'Hello, Claire,' Whitney said.

The pathologist gave her head a quick shake. 'You took your time, didn't you?'

'Hardly,' Whitney said, glancing at the clock on the wall. 'It's been no more than thirty minutes since we spoke.'

'The journey is only fifteen.'

'I had to collect George and there was a bit of traffic on the roads. Is that an issue?'

She resented being put on the spot like this. Most times she cut Claire some slack but today for some reason it was jarring.

'I was expecting you straight away. I do have other things to do,' Claire said.

'What is it you want to show us?' Whitney asked, fighting to keep her tone civil.

'Both victims died of smoke inhalation.'

'That's what the fire officer told us.'

'He combines pathology with fighting fires, does he?' Claire snapped.

'I was just saying,' Whitney held up her hands in mock surrender. 'He also said they weren't burnt.'

'That's correct. There were minor burns, but not enough to kill them. As the fire took hold it burnt the oxygen in the air. The more oxygen is removed from a room, the harder it is for a person to breathe. Not only that, due to the removal of oxygen all that's left is carbon monoxide, which is toxic.'

'So, what happened to them isn't out of the ordinary in these circumstances?' Whitney clarified.

'No, it's not. But there was some evidence of them having ingested drugs.'

Whitney went on alert.

'You mean someone drugged them and then set fire to the place?'

'I'm not sure if you can connect the two, but my investigation found there was evidence of drug taking. We won't know conclusively until the toxicology results come back, but I found frothy, blood-tinged fluid in both of their noses. That's indicative of them having taken a substance. I can't tell you whether it was voluntarily or not.'

'So, we still don't know whether it's murder or manslaughter,' Whitney said.

Nothing was sitting right. Claire was being extremely non-committal, which in itself wasn't unusual, but it was usually followed by a revelation of something far more interesting. It was the way the pathologist worked with them. It was like a game.

'Is there anything else? Surely you could have told me all this on the phone?' Whitney frowned. What was she missing?

'Actually, yes,' Claire said, clearing her throat.

This was getting more and more bizarre. In all the years she'd known the pathologist, she'd never once been so ill at ease.

'What is it?' Whitney exchanged a glance with George, who didn't appear to have noticed anything out of the ordinary.

'I got married at the weekend ...'

'You what?' Whitney spluttered, immediately hiding it with a cough, not wanting to upset her. Only Claire could make such an announcement while standing next to a dead body.

'Married. I wanted to let you know.'

Whitney clamped her jaw shut to stop it from dropping. She glanced at George, whose eyes now displayed a reaction. They'd known nothing of Claire's private life, apart from the fact she was single. She'd once mentioned a nephew, but that was the extent of it.

'Congratulations, Claire,' George said.

'I didn't even know you'd met someone,' Whitney said, pulling herself together. 'Congratulations.' She moved towards the pathologist, holding out her arms to hug her, but Claire took a step to the side. She and George were like peas in a pod. It was a good job most other people she knew were huggers, or she'd have a complex.

'We met online.'

She'd been on a dating site? Wow.

'Tell us about him. What's he like?' she asked, while George frowned.

Of course, she wasn't interested in all of this.

'He's a pathologist like me and works in Yorkshire.'

Whitney's heart sank. Did that mean Claire was leaving them? They'd been through that not long ago when the pathologist had contemplated taking another job. Whitney had been delighted when it never happened.

'How come you haven't told us about him before?'

'My private life is nothing to do with you.'

Whitney laughed out loud and Claire glared at her.

'Tell us about the wedding?'

'It was a quiet ceremony with close family.'

'I'm pleased for you. The three of us will have to go out for a celebratory drink.'

'Ralph wanted me to go out with my friends for a hen party, but I refused. It's not my thing, and there was no one I wanted to invite.'

'George and I would've come, if you'd have asked.'

'It's too late for that, now. The three of us going out for a drink would be nice, though. But not for a few weeks as I'm busy,' Claire said.

'If he works in Yorkshire, where are you going to live?' She had to ask.

'That's still up for discussion. I want to stay here but he likes working in Yorkshire.'

'You can't commute to Yorkshire, and he couldn't commute here,' George said. 'It's entirely impractical.'

You could always rely on George to point out the obvious. If left to Whitney, she'd have said that commuting was a perfect solution.

'It's not too bad on the train, I'm hoping to persuade him to find a position somewhere closer,' Claire said.

Knowing Claire as they did, he'd got no chance. He was bound to agree.

'So, tell us more. You met online and he's also a pathologist. What was it, a medical dating site?' Whitney asked, her curiosity getting the better of her.

'We didn't meet on a dating site. What a ridiculous suggestion. Do I look as though I'd go onto a dating site? We were both presenting at a conference and there were several online meetings we attended in the planning stages.' Claire stared at her like she was barking mad.

'How do I know? Anyway, I'm really pleased for you. What about your family, were they happy?' She might as well take the opportunity to find out as much as possible about Claire, as she suspected this would be her only chance. She'd never share again.

'There's only my mother. I have a brother who recently moved to New Zealand, so he didn't attend.'

'Is this the father of the nephew who stayed with you?'

'How do you know about that?'

'You told me.'

'Did I? I don't remember.'

'What about his family?'

'Some of them attended ... Stop asking me all these questions.'

'Where did you hold the reception?' Whitney asked, ignoring Claire's request.

'We had a meal in a hotel outside of the city. And that really is all I'm saying on the matter.'

'Well, congratulations, Claire. I'm really pleased for you,' Whitney said. 'I'll give you a call to arrange our drinks.'

'I'll wait to hear. You can go now.'

They walked out of the lab and, once out of earshot, Whitney burst out laughing, clutching at her sides.

George looked at her. 'You're being rather unkind,' she said.

'I'm pleased for her. Really, I am. It's just so strange. I never in a million years expected Claire to get married. It was sad that she had no one to invite to a hen party, though. We'll make it up to her when we go out for our celebratory drink, whenever that's going to be. And assuming Claire doesn't change her mind, as you know what she's like.'

'I don't think it's sad,' George said. 'It's simply a fact. If I ever get married, which I won't, I'd only have a few people to invite.'

'Me, too.' Whitney agreed. 'We're three sad cases. Anyway, let's get back to the station. We might need you tomorrow, if you're free. We're holding the press conference first thing and hopefully someone will have seen something which will help the investigation.'

SEVEN

Tuesday, 15 September

'Are you ready, Walker?' Jamieson barked from down the other end of the phone.

'Yes, sir.' Whitney gritted her teeth and shrugged on her jacket.

'We'll explain about the fire and say we're looking for any information. Let's make it short and sweet. I've got other things to do. Meet me at the conference room.'

'Yes, sir.' She pocketed her phone and left her office.

What did he have on which was so important? More paper to push?

Melissa, the force's public relations manager, was waiting outside the conference room and Whitney gave her a smile as Jamieson marched towards them.

'Come on, let's get this over with,' he snapped.

Whitney opened the door and, as usual, the room was full. Reporters sat at the front and camera operators were at the back. She recognised most of them as they'd been coming in for briefings for many years. They also tended to sit in the same seats. Usually, she hated press conferences, but the thought that this might be the last one they held in this building hit her. She swallowed.

'Thank you, for coming in,' Melissa said, once they were seated. 'I'd like to hand you over to Detective Superintendent Jamieson.'

She slid the mic over to him.

'I'm here to inform you that we have had two suspicious deaths as a result of a fire in Stanton Road on Sunday night. We are looking to speak to everyone who was in the area from ten at night until the early hours of the morning. All phone calls will be treated confidentially.'

'Do you have names for the victims?' one of the reporters called out.

'I'll hand you over to Detective Chief Inspector Walker and she'll answer your questions.'

He passed the microphone over to her, and she leant forward to speak into it.

'We're not releasing the names of the victims at this point, out of respect for the families,' she said.

There were a few groans but most of them nodded. It was Lenchester's policy to do so, unlike other forces who released names of the deceased almost immediately. Whitney supported the policy. It was hard enough to learn of the death of a loved one, without them having to navigate the media's onslaught. They showed no compassion towards the families of victims, only considering their bylines.

'How did they die?' a reporter in the front row asked.

'Smoke inhalation,' she said.

'How was the fire started?' another reporter called out.

'We're waiting for the fire officer's report, but it's believed an accelerant was used on a cloth and pushed through the letter box,' she said.

'Is there anything you can you tell us about the victims?'

She glanced at the young reporter sitting in the middle of the room. 'They were both aged twenty and students at Lenchester University.'

'Do you have any idea of motive?' he followed up.

'We're still investigating. We'd like anyone who was in the vicinity from ten Sunday night to get in touch with us, as Superintendent Jamieson has already mentioned. Also, if anyone believes they have information regarding the fire, please contact us in confidence. Thank you very much for your time.'

They left the conference room and Jamieson strode off, not bothering to wait for her, as he usually would. What was going on? Was he worried she might question him further about the forthcoming interviews? Or question him about his future plans?

She returned to the incident room where the team was working. It was unusually quiet, and even Frank – who could be counted on to be eating or talking to his wife – was studying his computer monitor. Obviously, she wasn't the only person unnerved by the upcoming interviews.

'We've just held the press conference and requested the public's help.' She walked over to the board. 'I still haven't heard back from the pathologist regarding the drugs in our victims' systems. Ellie, what else have you found out about the two victims?'

'Nothing out of the ordinary. I've contacted the university and asked for their academic records. Cara was studying liberal arts, and Hamish, history. They were both average students, achieving mainly C grades. I checked their social media accounts, and nothing stood out which indicated why they would have been chosen. Sorry.' She shook her head.

Ellie always felt bad if she couldn't produce some *research miracle* out of the bag and Whitney often had to reassure her that the job she did was excellent and she was a highly valued member of the team. How that would stack up in the reshuffle was anyone's guess.

'Guv,' Matt called out. 'I've got someone on the phone who witnessed something close to the area. He said that when he drove down the street in his car there was someone hanging around.'

'That's a quick response, we've only just held the press conference,' she said frowning.

'He said he saw the story on the Internet.'

'Ask him to come into the station as soon as possible.'

'Okay, will do.'

She took out her phone and called George.

'Hello,' George said, answering after only the second ring.

'We've got someone coming in who claims to have seen someone close to the fire. Any chance you can come in and observe the interview, to make sure he's genuine? You know what some of these pyromaniacs are like, trying to get involved in the case.'

'Sorry, no. I've got a meeting I can't miss.'

'No problem. We can handle it.'

'Anything else?' George asked.

'Nothing since yesterday.'

'Keep me informed. I'm busy so need to go.'

'Okay, speak to you again soon.' She ended the call wondering why her friend had been so dismissive. But, then again, this was George so she should be well used to it.

'Guv,' Matt called. 'Mr Newman has arrived. Do you want me to come with you to interview him?'

That was quick. Too quick. It was one thing to see the story on the web so quickly, but to be so close to the station at the exact time it was released? She didn't like it.

'Yes, we'll go together.'

They walked into the interview room and seated was a man who looked to be in his late forties with short grey hair, cut

53

tidily around his ears. He appeared very relaxed as he rested his hands on the table.

'Good morning, Mr Newman,' Whitney said. 'Thank you for coming in.'

'I saw online about the fire and you wanting people who knew anything to get in touch. I was around there on Sunday night, and that's why I'm here.'

'We appreciate that very much. I'm going to record our conversation as it saves taking notes, if you don't mind?'

'That's fine with me,' he said in his broad Lenchester accent.

She pressed the recording equipment. 'Interview taking place on September fifteenth. Those present: Detective Chief Inspector Walker and Detective Sergeant Price. Please state your name,' she said nodding to Mr Newman.

'Rex Newman.' He gave her an open-mouthed smile that made her skin prickle.

Whitney wished she'd got George with her because he was acting very smug, almost as if he was enjoying being part of their investigation. Was this a telltale sign of a culprit muscling in on an investigation?

'Thank you for coming to see us, Mr Newman. If you could run through exactly what you saw on Sunday evening.'

'I'd been visiting my friend Pat who lives close by and I was driving past on my way home. It—'

'Did you see the fire blazing?' Whitney interrupted.

'No, I didn't see the fire, or I would have stopped. But when I was driving past, I did see someone sitting on a low garden wall opposite the house, just staring at it.'

'Male or female?' Whitney asked.

'I'm fairly certain male.'

'Could you describe him?' she said.

'It's difficult to say because it was dark.'

'What time was it?'

'Around eight o'clock. My friend and I had got some fish and chips after we'd been out for the day. When we'd eaten, I drove home.'

'And you were driving slowly enough to make out a male sitting on a wall opposite the house which burnt down several hours later?'

He shifted awkwardly in his seat. 'I slowed down as I went past.'

'Why?'

'No reason.' He shrugged, but the smug gleam had gone.

Was he checking the man out? Definitely worth pressing for more information.

'How old would you say this person was?'

'Maybe in his early twenties. Could be younger. Could be older. I'm not actually sure.'

She bit back her frustration. 'What was he wearing?'

'I think he had a hoodie on.'

'Was the hood up or down?' she pressed.

'I'm not sure.'

'So, you saw a male sitting on the wall opposite at around eight in the evening. You're not quite sure what he looked like, but he might, or might not, have been wearing a hoodie with the hood up or down ... But it was definitely a male. Are you sure this person couldn't have been female?'

'I'm fairly certain the person I saw was male. The way he was sitting, leaning forward a bit with his legs splayed.'

'Did you by any chance take a photo of him with your phone?'

'No. Why would I have done anything like that? We're not allowed to use the phone and drive.'

This was getting them nowhere.

'What were you doing between eleven and one, on Sunday night?'

'I was at home by then, why?'

'Can anyone vouch for you?'

'No, I live on my own. But why is it relevant? I've come in to help, surely if I was the person who set the fire I'd be keeping well away from here.'

'You'd be surprised, Mr Newman, what criminals do.'

'It wasn't me. You could ask my neighbours if they saw my car in the drive at that time, then you'd know.'

She'd ask one of the team to follow it up.

'Thank you very much for your help, Mr Newman. At least we know we've got someone to look out for.'

'Is there anything else I can help you with?' he asked. 'I'm a law-abiding citizen and I want to help the police.'

Maybe he was genuine. She was inclined to think so.

'No, that's all for now. Thank you,' she said, casting a glance at Matt, frustrated that they were still no further in the investigation.

EIGHT

Seeing those flames shooting up into the air. Streaks of orange against the dark night.

Shit, that was sick. The crackles and bangs as the fire took hold. Awesome.

I didn't realise there was anybody home. It was a shock when I found out. But in a good way. It made the whole thing even better.

The elders will take notice of me now. They have to.

They might even use what I've done to show others.

I was only meant to do one fire. That was all they wanted.

But now I've done it, I don't want to stop.

Burning things in the garden is nothing now I've seen a house go up.

And when the fire service came screaming in, their sirens blaring, followed by the ambulance and police. Big yikes.

I'm glad I hung around long enough to see them bring out the bodies.

Did I feel guilty?

Are you kidding me?

I get even more bragging rights.
Next time there'll be more than two.
This is going to change my life forever.

NINE

Thursday, 17 September

Whitney opened the pizza box that had just been delivered and groaned at the smell of the melted cheese and tangy tomatoes. She was sitting in front of the television with a glass of wine waiting for her favourite TV programme, *A Place in the Sun*, to start.

She was envious of people who'd moved somewhere warm overseas. It was always something she'd fancied, but couldn't contemplate with her mum and brother, Rob, still depending on her. Her mum was in a care home as she had dementia, and her brother lived in an assisted care facility due to brain damage he received after an assault when he was a teenager. No way could she leave them. Nor would she want to.

But that didn't stop her spending an hour drooling over sandy beaches, lovely blue skies, brilliant sunshine, and quaint little fishing villages every so often. In an ideal world, when she retired, she would settle somewhere like Portugal. Or, maybe, even Australia if that's where Tiffany decided to stay.

It had been a heavy week and she'd been at work since six

that morning. She needed time to relax which is why, this evening, she'd planned to have some alone time.

She lifted out a piece of her meat lovers pizza and took a bite. Sharp peppers and smoky bacon exploded in her mouth. Food was so much better when someone else made it for you. Her phone rang and she glanced at it, sitting on the table. It was work. She let out a sigh. She'd have to answer it, even though she was off duty. She dropped the slice of pizza back into the box.

'Walker,' she said, trying to inject some enthusiasm into her voice.

'Guv, we've just had a call regarding another fire,' one of the longer serving desk sergeants told her, almost apologetically. 'We don't know if it's related but thought you should know.'

Her heart sank. Not another one. Did that mean they were looking at a serial arsonist? That was all she needed. It also meant she couldn't ignore it. She had to respond.

'Where is it?' she asked.

'It's at a small old factory building in Brook Street, in the city. It's currently being used by an amateur theatre group.'

She knew the street. It was fairly close to a residential area that rarely caused the police any trouble. If she ever had sufficient funds and motivation to move, it was a place she'd definitely consider.

'Was there anybody in the building when the fire took hold?'

She prayed the answer was no.

There was a long pause. 'As far as we're aware, yes. According to the person who phoned it in, tonight is the night the group rehearse.'

Damn. All she could hope for was that they'd all managed to escape unscathed.

'Any casualties?'

'Sorry, guv, I don't know.'

'Okay, I'm going there now.' She ended the call and took her pizza into the kitchen, her appetite suddenly gone.

Once she'd picked up her jacket and bag from the chair at the kitchen table, she left. In the car, she called Matt.

'Hi, Matt. Where are you?' she asked once he'd answered.

'I've just got home, guv. Is there a problem?'

'There's a fire at an old factory building in Brook Street. Any chance you can meet me there?'

'I'm on my way. I'll see you shortly,' he said, his tone bright and not sounding at all pissed off by being called out.

'Send my apologies to Leigh for dragging you away.'

'She understands, guv. It's part of the job,' he said, giving a hollow laugh. Whitney suspected his wife might not be as understanding as Matt was making out.

She pushed her old car as fast as it would go, guided by the thick clouds of smoke that reached high into the dark sky, shielding the moon and stars. The street lamps cast a dull light through the darkness and once she'd arrived, she hurried over to the cordon and held out her warrant card for the closest fire officer to see.

'Detective Chief Inspector Walker,' she said to him. 'Can you give me an update?'

He pulled back his protective gear, his face etched with worry lines. 'We've found twelve bodies but are still searching. There could be more.'

Twelve bodies. Nausea washed over her.

Twelve grieving families will have their lives destroyed. Sometimes she hated her job. If this was another case of arson, what sort of person could take so many lives without even a care for the consequences? Her stomach twisted.

'Any idea how the fire started?'

'Not yet, but when we arrived, the entrance was locked, so the people stuck inside couldn't get out.'

Her legs almost gave way. 'From the inside or the outside?' she checked.

'We don't know yet. That will come out in the investigation.'

'How were you notified about the fire?'

'We were called out by a passer-by.'

'Do you know who? Are they still here?'

'Sorry, I've no idea. The emergency service didn't tell us. But it will have been logged.' It was as if he thought she wouldn't be aware of the procedures. 'Eight of the bodies have been taken to the morgue and the others are waiting to go. We were lucky that it was possible to remove them all straight away.' He nodded in the direction of the factory, where she could see the victims lying covered on the floor. She hoped the ambulances would arrive soon.

'Okay, I'll leave you to it,' she said, letting out a long sigh. Once Matt arrived, they could get on with their investigation.

People had gathered around the perimeter, standing around watching. She took out her phone and videoed everyone as a precaution. Until they knew the cause of the fire, she would assume it was arson. The culprit may have stayed to admire their handiwork.

She pocketed her phone as Matt jogged over to her.

'Sorry, it took me longer than anticipated to get here, guv. What can you tell me?' he said.

'It's not good. So far, they've brought out twelve bodies. The fire officers are still in there searching. I hope there are no more. The door was locked so they couldn't get out. I've taken a quick look around, but we can't go close to the building yet. We'll talk to the onlookers and see if anyone saw anything. Let's split up, in case some of them decide to leave. You take the people over there.' She pointed to where there were several people huddled together. 'And I'll take those over here.'

'Okay, guv,' he said turning and heading in the direction of the group clustered to the right.

She hurried over to where there were two teenage girls staring at the building. She held out her warrant card. 'I'm Detective Chief Inspector Walker. How long have you been watching?'

'We've only just arrived,' one of the girls said, shivering and wrapping her arms around her middle. Neither of them had coats. 'We'd been to the cinema and were on our way back home when we saw the smoke. We decided to come over to see what was happening. It's bad isn't it?'

It beat her how people could want to come and witness something as tragic as this. But then again, if they could assist in the investigation ...

'Since you've been here, have you noticed anybody acting suspiciously?'

'What do you mean suspicious?' the same girl asked.

'Someone watching intently. Maybe filming what was happening,' she said.

'No, sorry. We didn't really look at the other people here. Can we go now? Our mums will be worried if we're late.' An anxious look passed between them.

She pulled out her notebook. 'What are your names and phone numbers?'

'Are we in trouble?' The girl who'd been doing all the talking grabbed hold of her friend's arm.

'No,' she said, to reassure them. 'But we may need to speak to you again.'

They gave their details and Whitney allowed them to leave. She then headed over to an older man who was standing on his own holding a small dog on a lead. She held out her warrant card. 'I'm Detective Chief Inspector Walker. How long have you been here watching?'

'I'm the one who called the fire brigade,' he said.

She went on full alert. That meant he'd been hanging around there for some time.

'And you've been here ever since?'

She glanced down at the dog who was sitting quietly by his owner's feet. How easy would it be to start a fire with a dog in tow? Then again, if people saw a man with his pet, it wouldn't raise alarm.

'Yes. I was waiting to see what had happened. They've brought out so many bodies. It's quite disturbing.'

Yet he didn't go home. Why not? Was it really that fascinating?

'At what time did you spot the fire?'

He glanced at his watch. 'Maybe an hour ago. I called the fire service straight away and it took ten minutes for them to arrive. The police and ambulance were here shortly after.'

'When you saw the fire did you attempt to go inside the building?'

He frowned. 'No, of course not. The flames had already taken hold. We're lucky the factory isn't closer to the nearby houses, or it could have been even more catastrophic.'

She retrieved her notebook from her pocket. 'What's your name?'

'Paul Redford.'

She wrote it down. 'And when you first noticed the fire, was there anyone hanging around?'

'Not that I noticed. I was walking my dog.'

She scanned the area. It wasn't the place she'd normally expect to see a dog walker. It didn't lead to any grassed areas for the dog to run around.

'Why did you come this way, it's not near any park areas?'

He hesitated. 'I wanted to get out of the house as I needed time to think. I ended up here.'

It seemed a lame reason. 'To think about what?'

'Stuff,' he said shrugging.

'Could you be more specific?' she asked.

'Work. Home. The usual.'

'I'd like your phone number and address, and also for you to come to the station in the morning so we can take a statement.'

He shifted awkwardly from foot to foot. 'What about work? I have to be there first thing.'

'Where are you based?'

'In the city, in Grafton Street.'

'That's not too far from the station. Come in before you start. I'll be there from seven-thirty onwards.'

After noting down his details, she glanced up and saw Matt heading in her direction. She went over to join him.

'Did you get anything useful?' she asked.

'Not really. All of the people I interviewed didn't arrive until after the fire had started and didn't see anybody hanging around. I've taken their contact details so we can follow up with them.'

'Good. I've been speaking to the man who phoned in the fire as he was still here. He said he'd been walking his dog at the time.'

'This far out of the way?' Matt said. 'It's hardly a dog-walking area.'

'That was exactly my reaction. When I pushed him on it, he told me he'd been out thinking, and had ended up here. I've asked him to come into the station tomorrow first thing. We'll take a proper statement from him then. I videoed everybody who was here when I arrived with my phone.' She looked at the building. Several fire officers were standing outside. 'Before we leave, let's go over and find out if there's anything else they can tell us.'

'Hopefully no more deaths,' Matt said.

They walked to the cordon and she beckoned over the officer she'd spoken to earlier. 'Any update?'

'We have found two more people who are both alive, but

unconscious. They were in a different part of the building. They've been taken to hospital.'

'Thank goodness there are no more deaths. We'll visit them in the morning and see if they're up to being interviewed. They might be able to shed more light on what happened. Any thoughts yet on cause?'

'Off the record, it looks like arson,' the officer said. 'But until the fire inspector has made his assessment we won't confirm officially.'

Not what she wanted to hear. 'Thanks.' She turned to Matt. 'I think that's all we can do for now. I'll see you tomorrow. Be in early.'

TEN

Friday, 18 September

Whitney arrived at her office at just after seven. Her insides clenched as the first email she opened listed the names of the twelve people who had lost their lives in the fire. She printed it off and headed into the incident room. The team had now arrived and the same discomforting quiet hung in the air. Was it going to be like that until everyone knew their fates? At least the investigation gave them something else to focus on.

She walked over to the board.

'Listen up, everyone,' she said, sticking up the list of names. 'As you know, there was another fire last night at a factory in Brook Street. Twelve people have died and there are a further two people in hospital. I've been informed that their injuries aren't critical, so I'm going to interview them later. Last night Matt and I spoke to people at the scene—'

'Rubberneckers,' Frank interrupted.

'Yes, I agree. But as much as we don't approve of their actions, they're the ones who can give us vital information. One of the people interviewed was the man who phoned in the fire.

He's coming in this morning to make a statement. He was walking his dog at the time, although it was quite a distance from where he lived.'

'Sounds iffy,' Frank said.

'It's something to consider and I'll be sure to discuss it with him further when he arrives. Ellie, his name is Paul Redford and he lives on Mountford Road. Look into his background. Family, friends, social media. The usual drill.'

'Yes, guv,' Ellie said.

'Do it now, as I'd like to have as much information as possible before he arrives. Doug, contact Rex Newman for an alibi. I know his neighbours confirmed that his car was at home during the time of the last fire, but that doesn't mean he didn't slip out using a different mode of transport.'

'Yes, guv,' Doug said.

'Frank, I want you to take a look at the CCTV footage from around the factory. There are plenty of cameras close by so we should be able to see if there was anyone hanging around prior to the fire being set.'

'Yes, guv. I've already been looking at it.'

Whitney stared at the older officer, impressed that he'd actually taken the initiative. Usually he waited for instructions. Was he worried about his job and trying to create a good impression? Was she even the right person to be impressing?

'Good work, Frank. What have you found?' She hurried over to his desk and stood beside him.

'There aren't any cameras focused on the factory itself, but these views were all taken from ones close by.' Frank pointed to the three different shots on his screen. 'These cover the time prior to the fire being reported. We don't know exactly when the fire was set, but there's no evidence of smoke so these are definitely earlier. As you can see, there's no one here. The street's empty.'

'Did you check footage from earlier? What time did members of the theatre group arrive?'

'Most of them were there by six, and there was one person who was fifteen minutes later.'

'Did you see anything else?'

'Around an hour before the shots on my screen, a man walking a small dog went past. This same man was there once the fire had started.'

It had to be Redford. Was he their arsonist? His story wasn't matching up with what Frank had found. She pulled out her phone and opened the video she'd taken last night. She paused the recording once she found Redford and his dog.

'Is this the guy?' she asked, holding out her phone for Frank to see.

'Yes, that's definitely him.'

Whitney let out a breath. Finally, they had a lead.

'What time was he near the factory the first time?'

'Seven o'clock.'

'Call it up on the screen.'

Frank pressed a few keys and in front of them was Redford. 'The time stamp is four minutes past seven, guv.'

'We now know he was close to the building at least an hour before the fire started, but that doesn't tie in with what he told me last night. Are you absolutely sure he walked away from the scene and wasn't just hiding out of the way of the cameras in order to set the fire?' She peered at the screen to check it was definitely him. No question.

'He didn't loiter the first time he walked past,' Frank said, pointing to the screen as the recording continued. 'You can see him heading up the street and away from the factory. He was walking fast.'

'Could he have doubled back and returned via a different street?'

'I doubt it. His image would have been picked up unless he

knew all of the camera angles and how to avoid them. I don't think it was him.'

'But he lied to us, and that still needs investigating. The factory was locked when the fire service arrived, but we don't know whether it was from the outside or inside. If it was outside, the arsonist could have done it to ensure maximum casualties.'

'Sick bastard,' Frank muttered.

'Are there any cameras angled so the front door to the factory is captured?'

'No, guv. Nor is there anything around the back, so we can't see if anyone set the fire from there, either.'

'Thanks, Frank. We'll have to wait for the investigation report to have it confirmed. I'll send you a copy of the video I took at the crime scene of everyone watching. Take a look and see if there's anything suspicious on there.' She headed over to Ellie's desk. 'After researching Paul Redford, I want you to find out who owns the factory and who has keys. I want to know if there was any reason for the door to have been locked while the drama group was rehearsing. Also, I'd like a rundown on the theatre group. Who's in charge. How often they rehearse. Anything that might be of some use.'

Although she'd given the young officer plenty of research, she knew from experience that it wouldn't take her long to come up with all the information she needed.

'Yes, guv,' Ellie said.

She returned to her office and reached for her phone.

'We've had another fire,' she said as soon as George answered.

'Oh, no.'

'This is much worse. Twelve dead and two in hospital, fortunately not critical. I'm going to visit the survivors in hospital later on this morning. Any chance you can join me?'

'I should be able to get away. Shall I come and pick you up?'

'Yes, please. Make it around eleven to give the hospital staff time to do their rounds. I'm expecting the man who phoned in the fire to come in first thing this morning to make a statement, and I want to speak to him before we go.'

'Okay, I'll see you at eleven.'

She replaced her phone on the desk and caught sight of Matt rushing towards her.

'Guv, Paul Redford's here. He's waiting in one of the interview rooms. Would you like me with you during the interview?'

'Yes. But first I want to check what Ellie's come up with.'

Whitney got to her feet and they both headed through the subdued incident room over to the far desk. Ellie looked up from her screen, eyes bright.

'Hi, guv. I was about to come and give you an update.'

'Good. Redford's just arrived.'

'He's married and works as a dentist. He has his own practice in Winterbourne Street and he's also a member of the local Rotary club.'

'Nice work. How did you manage to discover all of that so quickly?' Whitney was often in awe of Ellie's talents, but this time she'd excelled herself.

'It wasn't hard. He's big on social media,' the officer said, blushing.

She could never understand why people would want to put their whole lives on display for the world to see. It wasn't her thing at all.

'Hang on a minute. Did you say Winterbourne Street?' she checked.

'Yes, guv.'

'Last night he told me he worked in Grafton Street. Another lie. Thanks, Ellie. Come on, let's go,' she said turning to Matt, who'd been studying the folder in his hand. 'Our Mr Redford has a lot of explaining to do.'

She rushed out of the incident room with Matt following.

'What do you make of all the restructuring?' he asked as they stepped to one side to make room for a group of uniformed officers to go past.

They'd already spoken about it, so why was he asking her now?

'We have no choice but to accept whatever transpires. Why are you asking?'

'I'm thinking of accepting redundancy, if it's offered.'

She stopped dead and turned to him. 'You can't be serious. Why?'

'If I did, it would mean I could stay at home full-time with the baby.'

'I can understand initially you'll want to be at home, but taking redundancy is a huge step. Have you thought this through properly?'

'Leigh and I have discussed it at length and think it could work out for the best. It would mean that I'll be there for every step. I'll see her first smile. See her take her first step. See her—'

'It's a girl? That's amazing.' It was the first time he'd actually mentioned the sex of the baby. She thought they'd decided to keep it a secret.

'Crap. You didn't hear it from me,' he said, colouring slightly. 'It just slipped out. Don't mention I've told you if you speak to Leigh or she'll kill me. We've been so careful not to tell anyone.'

That wasn't going to be an issue, seeing as she rarely spoke to Matt's wife. Not because she didn't want to, but the couple had never been part of the police force culture, preferring to keep home and work lives separate.

'My lips are sealed. But make doubly sure that staying at home is what you really want. I thought both sets of parents were going to help so you could continue working.'

'We haven't made a final decision, but if the redundancy

package they offer is good, then we will definitely consider it. That doesn't mean I won't come back to work at a later stage.'

'It's your decision, obviously, but don't do anything rash. I'd hate to lose you. It wouldn't be the same around here without you.'

'Thanks, guv, but it's a difficult situation. Whatever I decide, it's not going to be the same going forward. We don't even know if you'll be here either after the reshuffle. You could be moved somewhere else.'

Her fists clenched by her side. 'Over my dead body. I can't move anywhere, not with Mum and Rob to consider. I'd sooner leave and become a PI.' She paused. 'That's a good idea. We'll both leave and set up a PI business. You could work around Leigh's shifts. A perfect solution.'

'Do you mean it?' Matt asked, frowning.

Did she? Or was it just a joke? She wasn't sure. Though it was definitely tempting. Especially the part where she no longer had to answer to men like Jamieson.

'Not at the moment, but it's an option. I'll wait and see after the interview and what's offered to me. In an ideal world, we'll all be able to carry on as we've always done. But, as George would say, that's me operating under the ostrich mentality. Back to you, though. Please don't do anything you might regret. At least not without discussing it with me first, or someone else if you'd rather not involve me.'

'I promise you'll be the person I consult. As far as work is concerned, I value your advice above anyone else's.'

They continued to the interview room. Paul Redford was dressed conservatively in a dark suit, pale blue shirt, and striped tie. He looked more like a bank manager than a dentist. He didn't appear fazed by being at the station.

'Thank you for coming in, Mr Redford. We'll record our interview as it's easier for us rather than taking notes.'

'No problem,' he said. 'I can't be too long, as I'm expected at work. It's a busy day, with back-to-back appointments.'

'Interview on Friday, eighteenth September. Those present, Detective Chief Inspector Walker and Detective Sergeant Price. Please state your full name,' she said nodding towards Redford.

'Paul Dominic Redford.'

'We'd like to go over what happened last night. You told me you were out walking your dog and were so busy thinking that you ended up walking further than you'd intended, ending up in Brook Street.' She paused. 'Is that what you still claim?'

'Yes, that's right,' he said, nodding.

Whitney looked at him. He couldn't quite meet her eyes. Even without George, she knew that was a sign of deceit. Of course, it helped that she was already aware he was lying to them. She'd get to that in a minute.

'We've been examining the CCTV footage in the area near the fire, and you were close to the factory at least an hour before you saw the blaze and called it in. Can you explain that?' He looked away and was silent for a while. 'Mr Redford,' Whitney prompted.

'This is really difficult. If I tell you something, can you assure me it will remain confidential?' He leant forward slightly, his eyes pleading.

She could hazard a guess at what he'd been up to but needed to hear it from him.

'It depends on what it is. I can't promise but if it's nothing to do with our investigation, then we'll try our best to keep it quiet. You need to tell us what you were doing as this is an arson attack we're investigating.'

'You think it was deliberate?' His brow furrowed.

Was he acting, or was he genuinely surprised?

'Yes, we do. This is the second fire we've had recently which means we could be looking for a serial arsonist.'

Damn. She didn't mean to say that. If he was involved, he shouldn't have been told. Then again, the first fire had already been reported in the media, so no harm would have been done.

'You're right. I was in the vicinity an hour before the fire, and then on my way back I saw it and called it in.'

'Why didn't you tell me this last night?'

'Because I'd been out visiting someone, and it wasn't something I wanted to publicise.' He glanced away.

'Why not?'

'Because my wife doesn't know.'

As she'd suspected. He was most likely meeting a lover.

'Why didn't you tell her what you were doing?' Whitney asked, not concerned whether it was difficult for him as all she wanted was the full story, to confirm her suspicions.

'Because I was meeting another woman,' he muttered.

'Can this woman vouch for you?'

'Yes, but I don't want her brought into it.'

'We need to eliminate you from our enquiries, and if this woman is the only person who can do that, then we will have to contact her.'

'Okay,' he said, letting out a sigh.

'I'd like to confirm with you, that you took the dog out for over two hours and your wife knew about this extended walk,' Whitney said.

Surely the wife would have thought something was odd. No one would take a small dog out for a two-hour walk at that time of night.

'When I left, my wife hadn't returned home from work. I left her a note saying that I'd taken the dog and that I'd see her later.'

'Didn't she think it strange that you were out in the dark?'

'No, I'm often out after dark. It's the time I do my thinking and planning for work.'

Work. That reminded her.

75

'Last night you told me you work in Grafton Street, yet we've discovered today that you actually work in Winterbourne and have a dental practice.'

He froze and stared at her. 'How do you know all this?'

'It's our job to know. So, how about you start telling the truth and not the half-baked version that you've given us up to now.'

'I didn't think you'd check. I said it so you couldn't trace me. It was a stupid thing to do, I wasn't thinking straight. I'm sorry.'

'I'm still not clear about it all, though. It must take you a long time to walk both ways, which means you couldn't have had much time together.'

'We didn't spend long in each other's company last night because I was on foot. Sometimes I catch the bus which gives us longer.'

'Always with the dog?'

If only animals could speak.

'Yes.'

'Write down this woman's details, and we'll contact her to confirm your alibi.' She passed over her notebook and watched as he wrote down the details. 'They had better be accurate.'

'They are,' he said, sheepishly.

'Good.'

'Do you need anything else from me?' he asked.

'Not for the moment. But we may be in touch again.'

ELEVEN

Friday, 18 September

George pulled up outside the station a few minutes before eleven and went upstairs to find Whitney. She was glad to get away from work for a while and immerse herself in something other than Ross's exhibition. Her constant thoughts about it were perplexing. She'd always been an expert at compartmentalising the various segments of her life, yet with this issue, she was unable to do so. She'd tried many times to push the thoughts aside, but they kept returning to the forefront of her mind. The situation was untenable if she was to work effectively.

She entered the incident room and was hit by how quiet it was. Not at all how she'd come to expect it to be. She couldn't see Whitney, so she walked through to her office. Whitney was on the phone but beckoned for her to come in. George stood by the door until the officer had finished her call.

'Sorry about that,' Whitney said. 'I had to let Jamieson know about the latest fire and what we were doing. Of course, he hadn't read the dailies so didn't know anything about it.

We've got twelve dead and two in hospital. It's an awful situation.'

'Have you learnt anything else yet?' she asked.

'No. The man who called the emergency services is a non-starter, despite him and his dog passing the factory over an hour before the fire was lit. It turned out he'd been visiting his mistress, which explained why he was so far away from home. Doug has just reported that Rex Newman, the guy who came in after the first fire, has an ironclad alibi for last night, which has been confirmed.'

'But he wasn't really on your radar though, was he?'

'No. But I didn't want to totally dismiss him until we were sure.' Whitney gave a loud sigh. 'Is it too much to ask for a case to be straightforward?'

'It's the nature of the job,' she said, shrugging.

'I was being facetious. I'm fully aware of what my work entails,' Whitney said, as she rolled her eyes.

George ignored it. She knew Whitney well enough to realise it was the way she aired her frustration. 'Hopefully the victims in the hospital will be able to help us.'

Whitney's phone rang and she picked it up. 'It's Claire. I'll put her on speaker. Hello.'

'I've got the drug results,' the pathologist said, as usual, dispensing with any pleasantries.

'George is with me, so you can tell us both.'

'Good morning, Claire,' George said.

'Right. Yes. Same to you. Toxicology found evidence of cocaine in the bloodstream of Cara Smythe and Hamish Ronson. Not enough to cause an overdose, so my conclusions are that it was taken for recreational purposes.'

'Thanks, Claire. Are you involved in the autopsies for the latest fire at the factory?' Whitney asked.

'Some of the bodies have been brought here, and others have gone to Rugby, as we don't have capacity to take them all.

If there's anything to report I'll let you know, although I suspect there won't be.' Claire ended the call.

'One day we might actually get a *hello* and a *goodbye* from her,' Whitney said grinning.

'I don't hold out much hope. Let's go to the hospital.'

Whitney picked up her coat and bag and they left, stopping on their way through the incident room to let her team know where she was going to be in case she was needed.

'Have you had any further thoughts about the exhibition?' Whitney asked as George turned out of the station car park and headed towards the hospital.

'It didn't take you long to ask,' she said, tossing a glance in Whitney's direction and arching an eyebrow.

'That's my job.'

Whitney had an emotional, idealistic streak and had expressed on several occasions how much she would love to see George and Ross get back together and ride off into the sunset. In real life those things didn't happen. Or if they did, it wasn't to George, or anyone else she knew.

'As you're so interested, I will tell you. I've decided that I am going to go.' She kept her eyes on the road ahead, not wanting to see the excitement in Whitney's eyes. It wouldn't be contagious but would probably make her want to change her mind. It hadn't been an easy decision to make and she wasn't one hundred per cent convinced it was the right one.

'That's fantastic. Would you like me to go with you, as we discussed?'

George strummed her fingers on the steering wheel. Initially, she'd thought it would be a good idea, but if she was going to spend some time with Ross, which was the whole point in her going, then it would be far better if she was on her own. At least that was how she felt about it today. The indecision was playing havoc with her sanity.

'I appreciate you offering, but I've decided to go on my own.'

'Are you sure you don't want any moral support?' Whitney said, a wistful tone to her voice.

She wasn't sure. But she'd shelved that thought at the back of her mind. She was making the best decision she could, under the circumstances.

'I don't want to make a big deal out of me being there because, for all I know, he won't be aware that I was sent an invitation. I'm sure he hasn't gone through the gallery's mailing list to check who's been invited. If he does see me and makes it clear he doesn't want me there, then I'll simply leave.'

The more she thought about it, the more she was wondering whether she was in fact making the wrong decision.

'I might have only met Ross a few times, but my instinct tells me there's no way he would be rude enough to *make it clear* he doesn't want to see you,' Whitney said.

'Yes, you're right. He isn't a rude person.'

'Let me know if you change your mind about me going with you. If we're both there, it might not be so awkward for you and Ross.'

'I don't follow your logic on that one. But I'm sticking with my decision to go on my own. How's it going with you?' she asked, anxious to move the conversation on from her. 'Do you have a date yet for your interview?' She glanced at Whitney, who grimaced.

'Not yet. I'm waiting to hear. It will be very soon, though.'

'Have you prepared for it?'

'Prepared? This isn't an exam. What preparation are you referring to?'

'Won't they want your opinion on performance indicators, the functioning of the new team, and the future direction of the force? Issues like that.'

'Yes, but it's not something I need to consider yet. I'll wait until my interview date is set and then make sure I have a full understanding of any policing issues they might ask me about. I've always been a crammer, leaving things until the last minute. Facts stick in my head better that way.'

Why didn't that surprise her? Occasionally, she wished for some of Whitney's impulsiveness. But certainly not when it came to something as important as a job interview.

'Not a good approach. What happens if an emergency crops up and then you can't prepare? Surely, it's better to do it in advance, to give yourself some breathing space.'

'We can't all be like you. I don't doubt that you've already prepared your lectures for the entire semester, the whole academic year, even.'

'There's nothing wrong with being prepared.'

'I was joking. Please don't tell me you really have prepared for the whole year, I already feel slapdash enough when compared with you.'

'The first two semesters, that's all,' she admitted.

Plus, most of the last, but she kept that to herself.

'You're seriously a machine.'

'It's the way I work. How are the rest of the team taking the restructuring? The atmosphere is very subdued. I was taken aback by how different it was in the incident room this morning when I arrived.'

'They're unnerved by the whole thing, understandably. Which isn't good as it makes working on the case harder. Everybody's on edge. It's like the elephant in the room all of the time. I've given them space and left them alone to discuss it whenever possible. They won't want me around, as I'm management, however well we get on.'

'I'm sure they don't hold you responsible for what's happening.'

'They don't, but it's a pain in the arse not being able to tell them exactly what's going to happen. I wish I knew. It's as bad for me as it is for them. All I can do is keep my fingers crossed that the team stays together. Or, even if it doesn't, that they all retain their positions, if they want them. Though realistically, that might not happen.'

'Is Frank likely to lose his job or be forced into retirement?' From an outsider's perspective, he seemed the most likely person to lose if they were looking to trim numbers.

'It could happen as he's a prime candidate,' Whitney said. 'He's not ready to retire yet, despite his slack attitude. Of course, since I've made the announcement, he's stepped it up a bit. Whether it's too little, too late, is anyone's guess.'

'What about Matt?'

'I don't know what's going to happen with him.' Whitney hesitated.

It seemed that her friend was hiding something, but she wasn't going to pry.

'And the others?'

'I'll be putting up one hell of a fight if they try to take Ellie away from me. She's worth two of any other researcher I've worked with. That's if I get to keep my job, of course. If I don't, then ...' Whitney's voice fell away.

'You'll be fine,' George said, wanting to reassure her.

She turned to see Whitney glaring at her. 'I'll pretend you didn't say that.'

TWELVE

Friday, 18 September

When they arrived at the hospital, they headed up to the reception and George stood beside Whitney while she showed her warrant card to the woman behind the desk.

'Can you tell me where I can find the two survivors from last night's fire?' Whitney asked.

'Yes, they're on Jupiter ward, third floor,' the receptionist said, without having to consult her records.

George supposed the woman must have already had plenty of enquiries about them from the media, though surely she'd had instructions not to tell anyone where they were.

They took the lift to the ward and stopped at the desk. 'I'm Detective Chief Inspector Walker. We're here to speak to Aimee Edwards and Gavin Curtis. Could you tell me where they are?'

'Aimee is in bed four, in the first room on the left, and Gavin is in bed three, in the second room on the left.'

They headed into Aimee's ward. She was the only patient. Her face was devoid of any colour and her straight blonde hair was splayed out across the pillow she was lying on. She stared up at the ceiling, seeming oblivious to their presence.

'Hello,' Whitney said as they walked up close. 'I'm Detective Chief Inspector Walker and this is Dr Cavendish. Do you feel up to having a chat with us about what happened last night?'

The woman pulled herself up slightly in the bed and coughed.

'Can I get you anything?' George asked.

'Some water would be good,' Aimee said, in between catching her breath.

George went over to the water cooler beside the sink, poured some into a plastic cup, and handed it to her.

'What do you remember about the fire?' Whitney asked, once Aimee's coughing had subsided and her breathing wasn't so laboured.

The woman glanced away, and bit down on her bottom lip. 'I don't remember much,' she said.

It was glaringly obvious from her behaviour, the inability to look at them and her guarded expression, that the woman was holding something back. Would Whitney notice? She was getting far better at interpreting body language these days, so hopefully she would.

'Nothing?' Whitney frowned and exchanged a quick glance with George. She clearly didn't believe the woman either. 'Didn't you realise the building was on fire before you became unconscious?'

'No. We ... we ...'

What wasn't she telling them?

'You and Gavin Curtis were found away from everyone else. That was most likely what saved your lives,' Whitney said, gently. 'Why weren't you with the others?'

'Gavin and I were talking,' she replied, her eyes focusing on the cup of water in her hand.

'In the middle of a rehearsal?' Whitney asked.

'We were having a break and decided to go off somewhere quiet for a chat.'

'Did you often disappear like that?' Whitney asked.

The woman blushed. 'Sometimes. What's happened to the other members of the group? Last night I gave the names of everyone who was in the building but no one will tell me anything. I've asked several of the nurses, but they said they don't know. What are they hiding?'

Was Whitney going to tell her? It wouldn't be hard to work out, seeing as other than the person she was found with there was no one else on the ward who was at the factory.

'Well ...'

'They didn't make it, did they?' the woman said, pre-empting whatever it was Whitney was going to say.

'No, I'm sorry, they didn't,' Whitney said.

She gasped. 'Oh no ... What about Gavin? If I've made it out alive, then surely he has, too.' Her eyes darted from Whitney to George.

'He's okay. He's in the next room,' Whitney reassured her.

The woman breathed a sigh of relief. 'Oh, thank goodness. I'm devastated about the others, but if he'd have died, too. I don't think ... think ...' Her voice fell away.

'What exactly were you and Gavin doing when the fire started?' Whitney asked.

'We'd gone to one of the offices at the far end of the building, away from the rehearsal area.' She paused. 'We wanted to talk.'

'So, you've already said. Are you sure you were only talking?' Whitney pushed.

Guilt flashed across Aimee's face and she looked down at the cup in her hand. 'Look, my husband ... Dale ... he mustn't know. It would destroy him.'

Now George understood. Whitney had obviously reached the same conclusion, only ahead of her.

'It isn't our intention to interfere in your marriage, however, we believe this might be the work of an arsonist and we have to investigate all possibilities regarding why the factory was chosen. When the fire service arrived at the scene, the door to the entrance was locked. Did you know about that?'

'Yes, our director decided to keep the front door locked because recently we'd been disturbed by people wandering in from off the street. Mainly kids. Is that why everyone died? Because the fire was at the side of the building and they couldn't get out of the front?' A sob escaped her lips. George reached for the box of tissues on the side and passed it to her.

'We won't know until the fire officer's report comes back and we find out where the fire started. It does appear to be likely though.'

'I can't believe it. If only we hadn't locked the front door, they might still be alive.' She leant back against her pillow, tears trailing down her cheeks.

'How long had you been locking the door?' Whitney asked, after pausing for a while, allowing the woman to regain her composure.

'About six weeks, I think.'

Did the arsonist know the door would be locked? Had they been observing the building for some time before deciding when to set it on fire? Choosing a time when it would cause maximum impact.

'Was the whole of the building locked?'

'No, only the main entrance. We've all been walking around to the side of the building once we arrive.'

'So, you park in the street and then go around the side. Is there a car park behind the factory?' Whitney asked.

'There is, but we don't use it because it's pitch-black and there's no lighting.'

'Which part of the building do you specifically use when you're there?'

'We rehearse in the old factory space as it's large and enables us to split off into separate groups if we need to work on individual aspects of the play.'

'I know this is hard for you, but we need to know what you remember.'

The woman tilted her head to one side and glanced upwards. 'We had gone into the office area of the building which was away from the main factory area. We were talking and after a little while, maybe ten minutes, we could smell smoke. Gavin tried to open the door, but the handle was hot, and he burnt himself. The smoke was seeping through from under the door. We ran to the back of the office and took cover under one of the desks. After that, I don't remember anything.'

'The smoke had got into your respiratory tract, causing your airway to collapse. You are both lucky to be alive. Being at the rear of the office, and far away from the fire, most likely saved your life,' George said.

'Not so lucky for the others, though,' Aimee said, shaking her head.

'No,' George agreed.

'Aimee, are you and Gavin in a relationship?' Whitney asked.

The woman nodded. 'Yes,' she said quietly.

'How long has this been going on?' Whitney asked.

'Six months.'

Not casual.

'Where is your husband at the moment?' Whitney asked.

'He called in earlier after taking our daughter to school and then he went down to the café to get something to eat as he missed breakfast. He said he'll come back after he's eaten.'

'Is he on his own?' Whitney asked.

George assumed that Whitney would want to interview

him. Could he have had something to do with the fire? It was possible if it was done in a fit of rage after finding out about his wife's infidelity.

'As far as I know. May I see Gavin?' she pleaded.

'You'll have to ask the doctor whether he's allowed visitors apart from members of his family. Certainly not yet, because that's where we're going next. We may need to speak to you again.'

'Promise you won't mention anything to Dale when you see him.'

'It isn't our intention to inform him of your relationship with Gavin, but obviously this is an investigation and we've got many deaths to deal with. Our priority is solving the crime. I can't promise that he won't eventually find out.'

Whitney and George left the room and stopped in the corridor when out of earshot.

'It was most fortuitous, that they were away from the fire,' George said.

'We need to consider that the fire could have been started by one of their partners if they'd known about the relationship,' Whitney said.

'If that's the case, we need to ascertain how it fits in with the first fire.'

'A diversion. It's not unheard of,' Whitney said. 'Especially if they believed the first property was empty. I'll ask Ellie to check if there's any link between the partners of Aimee and Gavin and the property in Stanton Road. Come on, let's see our other victim and then go to the café to find Dale Edwards.'

They hurried to the next room, where there were three men and one empty bed. On the wall above each bed was a number. Number three was beside the window, so they headed over there. The man was sitting up and looked a lot healthier than Aimee, apart from the bandage on his hand. His cheeks had some colour and his brown eyes were alert.

'Gavin Curtis?' Whitney asked.

'Yes.'

She made the introductions and said, 'We'd like to talk to you about last night.'

'I'm not sure if I can tell you anything as I passed out from the fumes. When we first realised there was a fire, I tried to open the door of the office where we were but couldn't because of the heat.' He held up his bandaged hand. 'I've asked the hospital staff about the others in the theatre group, but they wouldn't tell me anything.'

George drew the curtain around the bed and Whitney threw her a grateful glance. Though she wasn't sure whether it would make much difference as the other men in the ward would probably be able to hear them. Hospital wards provided little privacy.

'I'm sorry to tell you that you and Aimee Edwards were only two survivors from the fire.'

His jaw dropped. 'They're all dead?'

'Yes. I'm sorry.'

'That's ... that ...' His voice faded. 'But Aimee's okay, you said? Are you sure?' he asked, panic showing in his eyes.

'Yes. She's fine. We were talking to her a few minutes ago in the ward next door.'

He leant back against his pillow and exhaled a breath. 'Thank goodness. I couldn't imagine life without her.'

'We understand that you and Aimee have been having a relationship, and the reason you weren't with the others at the time the fire broke out is because, during the break, you'd gone off together.'

'She told you?' He glanced at George and then back to Whitney.

'Are you married?' Whitney asked.

'Separated. I'm back living with my parents, unfortunately, as I didn't have anywhere else to go when we split. But it won't be for long. Once I have some money, I'll move out. The ex-wife has the kids and the house. I don't begrudge her as she has the children to look after. It's amicable between us. When I have somewhere to live, they'll stay with me sometimes.'

'How long have you been having a relationship with Aimee?' Whitney asked.

'We've known each other for a few years from the theatre group, and it developed recently. About six months ago she came to rehearsal upset as she'd been having trouble with her husband. We talked and one thing led to another.' He shrugged, a sheepish expression on his face.

'She didn't mention issues in her marriage,' Whitney said, frowning.

'She wouldn't because she's too embarrassed.'

'Do you know the precise nature of these problems?'

'He has a gambling problem and took some of her jewellery to pay for his debts. She would have left him long ago if it wasn't for her daughter. Once I have somewhere, she's going to bring her daughter and move in with me.'

'Do you think Aimee's husband knows about the two of you?'

'No. We're very careful. No one is aware of our relationship.'

'What about others in the theatre group? Did you often disappear on your own to *talk*?' Whitney asked.

'They didn't know. Yesterday was the first time we'd gone off like that. Usually, we manage some time together later in the evening, after rehearsal, but Aimee said she had to get home because she was expecting a phone call. That was why we decided to take a few minutes to ourselves.'

'You were lucky,' Whitney said.

'We were, but not the others.' He shook his head. 'Is there anything else I can help you with?'

'Not at the moment, but we will be in touch,' Whitney said.

They left the ward and went into the corridor.

'Shall we go back to speak to Aimee?' George suggested.

'No, let's visit the hospital café to find her husband. If he did know about the affair, then he could have been the one to set the fire. Or, if a life insurance policy was taken out on her, he might have wanted her out of the way as it would help fund his gambling, and pay off any debts.

THIRTEEN

Friday, 18 September

Whitney and George walked into the hospital café to find Dale Edwards.

'I hope he's still here,' Whitney said as she scanned the large eating area, which had a mix of square and round tables, all with four chairs around them. There was a self-service counter at the back, and only two people waiting to pay.

The café wasn't too full. Two nurses were seated at one table, and an older couple at another. Towards the back was a man sitting on his own. He had short, medium brown hair and was wearing black jeans and a moss green crew-necked jumper.

'That could be him,' George said, nodding towards the table.

'He's the only man on his own, so you're probably right,' Whitney replied.

They approached the table, but he didn't appear to notice them. He was staring out into space, an empty plate in front of him, and his hands wrapped around a mug of coffee.

Whitney inhaled as the aroma reached her. Her whole body screamed out for caffeine. It seemed ages since her last coffee.

'Dale Edwards?' Whitney said.

He looked up, concern in his pale grey eyes. 'Yes. Who are you? Is Aimee okay?'

'I'm Detective Chief Inspector Walker and this is Dr Cavendish, who works with the police on certain enquiries. We've come from speaking to your wife and she told us you were here. We'd like to have a chat with you regarding last night's fire.'

'Okay,' he said, nodding. His face was lined and there were bags under his eyes. She suspected he'd had hardly any sleep last night.

They sat opposite him at the table.

'What do you know about the fire at the factory?' Whitney asked.

'Nothing, until the hospital called me last night. They said I couldn't see Aimee at the time because she was unconscious, so I came in first thing this morning, after taking my daughter to school. I understand a lot of people died and she was bloody lucky.'

'Yes. She was in a different part of the building and fire officers managed to get her out. They were only able to save her and one other person,' Whitney said.

'Yes, it was Gavin Curtis.' A dark shadow across his face, and his body tensed.

'You know him?' Whitney tossed a knowing glance in George's direction.

'Not to speak to, but I ... I ...' His voice fell away.

'What were you going to say?' Whitney asked.

'It doesn't matter,' he said, giving a dismissive flick of his hand.

'I'll be the judge of that,' Whitney said. 'Please continue.'

'I thought that Aimee was a lot friendlier with him than

most of the others in the group.' His hands balled into such tights fists that his knuckles went white.

'Could you be more specific?'

'I've seen them together. They appeared very *close,* for the want of a better word.'

She forced herself to remain objective and ignore the sympathy she was feeling for the man. It can't have been easy for him to witness such behaviour.

'When did you observe this?' Whitney asked.

'The times when I've watched the productions. There were secretive looks between them. They always ... It doesn't matter. It's not important. The main thing is they're still alive. That's all I care about.'

'Have you mentioned your suspicions to your wife?' George asked.

Whitney glanced in her direction. Had she spotted something she wanted to pursue?

'Things have been strained between us recently and I didn't want to add to it,' he replied, shifting awkwardly in his seat.

'What are the issues between you?' Whitney said.

The gambling?

'I fail to see why this is relevant. What goes on in my marriage isn't anything to do with the fire.'

'That's for us to decide,' Whitney said, an edge to her voice. She understood that he was distraught, but that didn't mean she would excuse him from giving her the information she needed. 'Please answer the question.'

He gave a sigh. 'I had some debts and needed to get hold of some money quickly, so I sold some items belonging to my wife without asking her first.'

'What sort of debts?'

He averted his eyes. 'From gambling.'

'What were the items of hers that you sold?'

'Several pieces of her jewellery. She didn't speak to me for a week after I'd done it. I apologised, but what else could I do? It was the last resort. I couldn't risk the guys I owed money to coming round to the house. Anything could have happened. They might have harmed Aimee and our daughter.'

'Are you now debt free?' Whitney asked,

Could loan sharks be responsible for the fire? She doubted it, but the question was worth asking.

'Yes.' He averted his gaze.

'Are you sure?' she checked.

'All I owe is a couple of hundred pounds, and I'll have enough money next week to pay it off.'

'There are organisations out there that can help with addiction,' Whitney said.

'I know. The fire has made me re-evaluate my life. When Aimee comes home from hospital, I'm going to book an appointment and sort myself out.'

'Going back to the suspicions you had of your wife and Gavin Curtis. Did you pursue them?' Whitney asked.

His brow knitted together. 'A couple of times I waited in my car after rehearsal was over to see where she went.'

'Didn't she come home straight after?' Whitney asked.

'They all go out for a drink once they've finished. I wanted to check if she went with them.'

'And did she?'

'Yes.'

'What about your daughter, did you leave her alone?'

'It wasn't for long.' He couldn't meet Whitney's eyes.

'How old is she?'

'Twelve.'

Not old enough to be left alone, in her opinion.

'Does she know you sometimes go out?' Whitney pushed.

'If she's awake, I tell her I've run out of cigarettes and won't be long.'

Whitney shook her head. Leaving a twelve-year-old alone

wasn't illegal, but even so, it wasn't something she would condone.

'What were you doing last night between the hours of seven and nine?'

Again, he couldn't quite meet her eyes. 'I was at home.'

'Can anyone vouch for you?'

'My daughter. But she's distressed enough with her mum being in the hospital. I don't want you talking to her.'

'What were you doing?'

'I watched the TV and did some work in the garage.'

'What sort of work?' Whitney asked.

'I own a small car repair business and operate out of a garage which backs onto our house.'

There would no doubt be plenty of items in there which could be used as an accelerant.

'We'd like to come and take a look,' Whitney said.

'Why?' he asked frowning.

'We're treating the fire as suspicious. At the moment, we're unsure whether the arsonist was targeting an individual person, or persons, or their interest was the building. We're investigating all possibilities.'

'Don't you need a search warrant?'

'If you've got nothing to hide, then I'm sure you won't mind,' Whitney said. 'We just want to take a quick look around and to have a further chat with you.'

'Surely you don't think it was me? I love my wife and would never do anything to harm her.'

'Even though you suspected her of having an affair?' She locked eyes with him.

'It wasn't me,' he said, banging his hand on the table so loudly that all conversation in the café stopped and people stared in their direction.

'I think we should continue this conversation elsewhere,'

Whitney said. 'You choose. Either at your house, or down at the station.'

'I've got nothing to hide,' he said, his mouth set in a flat line.

'Good. Once we've looked around, it should help exclude you from our enquiries,' Whitney said. 'What's your address?'

'I live at 36 Cheriton Street.'

'We'll meet you there,' she said.

'Aimee is expecting me to go back up to the ward.'

'You can go after we've been to your workshop,' Whitney said.

He finished his coffee and they left the hospital together, separating when they reached the car park.

'Don't you want him to come in our car?' George asked once they were alone.

'No. I doubt he's going to do a runner as he has his daughter to consider. All we want to do is look through the garage. Let's keep it as relaxed as possible. Currently, we have nothing tying him to the fire and we'll arrive at his house at the same time so he's not going to have time to hide any evidence ... that's if there is any.'

They arrived about thirty seconds before Dale Edwards and waited in George's car until he drove down the drive and parked in front of the garage.

'My workshop's in here,' he said, using a remote to open the door.

They followed him into the tandem garage. Lining the walls on both sides were tools on hooks. There was a ten-foot long bench running along the back wall. It reminded Whitney of her father's garage. When he was alive, he had every possible tool a person could want. He was a DIY expert.

'You're not working on anything at the moment?' Whitney said, glancing around the empty garage.

'No. I'm due to collect a car and bring it in for a service later this afternoon.'

'You mentioned that last night you were in here. What were you working on?'

'I was cleaning my tools. It's what I do every evening.'

Whitney headed towards the bench, skirting around the engine pit and the gas bottle next to it. Beside the bench was a large container with a pump attached.

'What's this for?' she asked pointing at it.

'It's oil,' Edwards replied.

On the bench was a bottle of paint thinner. Another accelerant. There wasn't much else in there.

'Thank you for letting us in here. We'd now like to look around your house, if you could show us,' she said.

'You didn't mention that,' he said, scowling.

'Is it a problem?' Whitney asked.

'No, I suppose not. But don't expect it to be tidy as I haven't made the bed or cleared up after my daughter's breakfast.'

'That's fine,' Whitney said. It sounded much like her house every single day.

'It's through here.' He opened the connecting door on the left which led them into the small kitchen. Plates and glasses were stacked up on the side and dirty saucepans filled the sink. He wasn't joking when he said it was a mess. Surely that couldn't be from just one night without Aimee being there. They must be as messy as each other. Yet he kept his tools clean. Interesting.

The door from the kitchen led into an open-plan lounge and dining area and there was another door that opened into a front porch. On every surface there were piles of laundry. Newspapers were stacked high on the coffee table.

The stairs went up from the lounge. As they reached the top Whitney turned to him. 'Mr Edwards, do you have life insurance?'

His eyes darted from Whitney to George. 'Why?'

'Do you?'

'Yes. We both do.'

'When did you take the policy out?'

'Last year.'

'Who is the beneficiary of your wife's policy?' Whitney asked.

'I am, and she is for mine.'

'How much were the monthly payments?'

'Fifty pounds?'

'Did you think of cancelling as you have debts?' George asked.

'No, as I didn't want to risk my wife finding out what I'd done. This is our bedroom.' He stepped forward and pushed open the door. Again, a mess, with an unmade bed and clothing littering the floor.

Whitney headed to the dressing table. One of the drawers was locked.

'Do you have a key?' she asked.

'No.' He hung his head. 'My wife keeps her jewellery in there and the key is with her all of the time.'

Wise move.

They continued looking, but aside from the equipment in the garage that could be used to start a fire, there was nothing which raised a red flag, other than the usual cleaning products.

'Thank you very much for your cooperation,' Whitney said as they headed downstairs. 'You mentioned that last night you stayed at home watching television. What did you watch?'

'I can't actually remember. I fell asleep.'

'What were you watching before then?' she pushed.

'I don't know. I didn't pay much attention. If you've finished, I've got work to be getting on with.'

'I thought you didn't have anything until you collect the car this afternoon.'

'I've still got my admin to do and I want to head back to the hospital to see Aimee.'

He showed them out and when they reached George's car Whitney stopped and glanced back at the house.

'He's got two motives. The debts and the affair. But do I think he did it? Call it gut instinct ... but no, I don't think he did.'

'Gut?' George said, rolling her eyes. 'Don't get me started on that.'

'You can say what you want ... I trust my gut. Come on, let's get back to the station. I'd like you to talk to the team about arsonists, and I need a coffee.'

FOURTEEN

Friday, 18 September

When they returned to the incident room, Whitney walked over to the board and under the names of Aimee and Gavin she wrote Dale Edwards. She turned to face the team.

'We've got two fires, and fourteen people dead. The first fire, the arsonist might not have known that the students were there. This means we have to consider whether that fire was set simply to put us off the scent. Fire number two, in the factory where the theatre group were rehearsing, only two people out of fourteen survived. These two people had been having an affair and were separated from the group at the time the fire started. They're currently in hospital suffering from smoke inhalation, but other than that are unharmed.' Her gaze settled on Frank. His head was bent over, and he was studying his screen. 'Frank. Is there a problem?'

'Sorry, guv. I was looking at something.' He nodded at his screen. 'There was a car close to the area. It circled back a few times and then parked close to the entrance. It left once the fire had started.'

Whitney's heart skipped a beat. This could be the lead she was hoping for. And it had come from Frank without her even asking.

'Does anyone get out of the car?'

'No guv. They stay inside.'

'Are you able to see the number plate?'

'Yes, and I'm about to run it through the database,' Frank said.

'Good. We've interviewed the husband of the woman who survived, and he did suspect that she was having an affair. We've been to his house and workshop, and there were plenty of things there which could have been used to start a fire. His name is Dale Edwards. He's a gambler and has debts. The couple also have life insurance. Ellie, I want you to find out what you can about him, and also our two survivors. Aimee Edwards and Gavin Curtis.'

'Yes, guv.'

'Before you do that, Dr Cavendish is going to tell us a little more about the type of person most likely to commit arson.' She turned to George and nodded for her to step forward.

'There are certain things we know about arsonists that need to be considered.' George paused. 'They are usually young, and rarely over the age of thirty.'

'Wouldn't that rule out Dale Edwards?' Sue asked.

'I'm talking in general. There are always exceptions,' George said.

'Why do people commit arson?' Frank asked.

'There are several different motivators. Often, arson is committed by young people to be a nuisance. They do it for kicks. However, around five per cent of fires are malicious, very often as revenge. Another motivator is that the psychological make-up of the person committing arson predisposes them to act in such a way.'

'A pyromaniac you mean?' Doug said.

'Yes.'

'Is there anything else?' Whitney asked.

'Yes. Simply put, fires could be lit for criminal reasons.'

'Like getting rid of evidence or making false insurance claims?' Frank said.

Whitney blinked. Usually Frank only made quips during their meetings.

'Exactly. We have to examine all of these different possibilities together. But, despite all that I've said, it's important to remember that most fires are set through boredom and thrill-seeking. In other words, they come under the 'nuisance' category. In the UK about eighty per cent of all cases of arson are spur of the moment, targeting empty properties such as schools or cars.'

'Going back to the profile of an arsonist, what else can you tell us?' Whitney asked.

'Of those arson cases which have been solved, half of the arsonists were male and under eighteen. The majority of the remainder were male and under the age of thirty,' George said.

'So, we should assume our arsonist is male and young,' Whitney said.

'It's worth bearing in mind, but not at the expense of other possible culprits,' George said. 'There has been quite a lot of research done on arson psychology, but as with most research, it's not all clear-cut. Another factor in our equation is that the majority of arson attacks are committed when it's dark. And, most importantly for us, not many arsonists are caught.'

Whitney's heart sank. That wasn't what she wanted to hear.

'Guv, I've just heard about the owner of the car hanging around. It belongs to Dale Edwards.' Frank called out.

Her despondency evaporated. Edwards had lied and now they'd got him.

'He didn't mention being there last night. I think that's grounds to bring him into custody. First, I'll get in touch with

Jamieson and ask for a search warrant. Once we have that, Matt, I want you to bring him in for questioning.'

'Yes, guv.'

She pulled her phone from her pocket and hit speed dial for Jamieson.

'Yes, Walker,' he said, answering straight away.

'We've got a suspect, sir. His name is Dale Edwards and he lives at 36 Cheriton Street. He's the husband of one of the survivors of the second fire. I'd like a search warrant, as soon as possible, for his home and work which are at the same address. I've already taken a cursory look, but we need SOCO and a search team in there.'

'Leave it with me,' he said, ending the call.

Whitney turned to George. 'It looks like we've got ourselves a strong lead. Let's grab something to eat while we wait for the warrant and for him to be brought in.'

* * *

George was discussing Whitney's forthcoming interview with her, as she'd just received notification of the date, when the officer's phone rang.

'Walker,' Whitney answered. 'Okay, we'll be down shortly.' She ended the call and placed her phone back on the desk. 'Edwards is here. I'll take Matt with me to interview, and you can watch from outside.'

'Why don't you use Frank?' George recommended.

'He's better at checking the CCTV footage and it's what he enjoys doing most. Why did you suggest him?'

'I remember him interviewing with you once before and I was impressed by how he did. He was able to predict the correct time to interrupt and obtain information from the suspect.'

Whitney's team ran well, and they each had their specialties, but it didn't do any harm to occasionally change things around.

'Okay, Frank it is. As we don't know how the restructure is going to pan out, it might go in his favour if he had more experience. Having said that, I'm leaving it a bit late for it to make a difference. Do you think having members of the team specialising in certain tasks makes them more vulnerable?' She turned to George, worry in her eyes.

'I can't speak for the selection panel, but in my opinion, it should help in keeping them together. You have built a successful team, with superb results. No one can argue with that.'

'Yes, but who knows how these paper-pushers think. If they're anything like Jamieson, their selection criteria may be totally different from mine.'

'Performance would have to be considered, whoever was doing the assessing. You will certainly be scored highly on that.'

Whitney gave a hollow laugh. 'For once, it's you being optimistic and not me. I hope you're right. I wish it was all over and done with, so we can make plans for the future.'

'You have my full support. If you would like me to write a reference for you, I'd be more than happy to do so.'

'It's very kind of you to offer, but selection panels in the force don't operate like that. Come on, let's go interview Edwards.' They headed into the incident room. 'Matt, has the search warrant come through yet?'

'Yes, guv,' her sergeant said, looking up from his desk.

'Good. Take Doug and Sue. Contact SOCO and ask them to meet you there.'

'Will do.' Matt removed his jacket from the back of the chair and slipped it on.

'Frank, would you like to come with me to interview Dale Edwards?' Whitney asked.

It was unlike Whitney to give her officers a choice, she

usually delegated, and they did as they were asked. Presumably because they trusted her judgement.

'Yes, guv.' He pushed his chair back and stood, his chest thrust out.

She'd been correct in advising Whitney to use him.

After arriving at the observation room, George noted the way Edwards was tapping his foot against the floor, clearly showing his discomfort. His eyes dilated and mouth flickered with uncertainty as Whitney and Frank entered the room.

'Why am I here?' he asked, before Whitney and Frank had time to sit down.

'We have a few more questions for you.' Whitney placed the folder she was holding on the desk. 'This interview will be recorded.' She leant over and pressed the record button, going through the usual protocol.

'I have nothing more to add after our last discussion,' Edwards said.

'We have a search warrant to search your home and work-shop and our team is executing it at present.'

'You can't do that without my permission.'

'He's hiding something,' George said. 'His fists were clenching and unclenching in his lap when you told him. You probably can't see it from your angle.'

'Yes, we can as we have a warrant.'

'B-but you've already looked through the workshop and house. I gave my permission then. You didn't tell me you would be going back. I—'

'Stop,' Whitney said, sharply. 'The search is going ahead, and there's no need for further discussion.'

He stared at Whitney, fear etched across his face. 'I want to be there.'

'That's not possible.'

'Why not?'

'Because I say so,' Whitney barked.

'Take a breath,' George said. 'He's scared. You snapping at him won't help.'

George wanted to help Whitney, who wasn't acting as she normally would, probably because of the impending restructure and what was going to happen to her staff. It was interfering with the way she operated. George hoped her comment would prompt the officer to reflect on her behaviour and act appropriately.

'Mr Edwards, we've been looking at the CCTV footage near to the factory around the time of the fire. Your car was seen driving around and then it was parked close by.' He couldn't meet her eyes. 'What were you doing there? You told us earlier that you stayed in last night watching the television.'

'I-I ...'

'You have become a person of interest as we now have evidence that you were close to the building before the fire was started. This is coupled with the fact that we know you have plenty of products in your workshop that can be used as an accelerant.'

Silence hung in the air as Edwards gazed upwards, clearly processing Whitney's comments and deciding what to say next.

'I admit to being out last night, but that doesn't mean I was the one who set the fire. I'd never do anything like that.'

'Why were you near the building?' Frank asked.

'Because I wanted to see them.'

'Who?' Frank asked.

'My wife and Gavin Curtis. I wanted to see if they left together and, if they did, I was going to follow them.'

'Why?' Frank asked.

'She knows,' Edwards said, nodding at Whitney.

'*She*. Show a little respect for the DCI.' Frank growled.

Edwards flinched and nodded his head by way of an apology. 'I suspected they were having an affair. I was going to follow them.'

'Have you followed them before?' Frank asked.

'Yes. As I explained earlier to the DCI.'

'According to the CCTV footage you left immediately after the fire had started. Why?' Whitney asked.

He hesitated. 'I just did.'

'Let me get this straight,' Whitney said, leaning forward, with both hands on the table. 'Your wife was in a building where a fire had started, and you did nothing about it. Instead, you left the vicinity and returned home.'

Edwards blinked furiously.

'He's rattled. I suspect what he tells you now will be the truth,' George said into the mic.

'I was about to call 999, I promise. But then I heard the fire engine sirens and knew someone else had.'

'You're not making any sense,' Whitney said. 'You claim that your wife was having a relationship with someone else and you wanted to find out for certain. Presumably, you still love your wife, otherwise you wouldn't be so angry about it. But when a fire started in the building she was in, you didn't attempt to rescue her. Instead, you left.'

'I know it doesn't make sense to you, but it did to me at the time. I went home and hoped it was going to be okay. I had my daughter to think about. I couldn't leave her on her own for much longer.'

George turned as Ellie walked into the observation room.

'I've got a message for the guv,' the officer said in a low voice, even though no one in the interview room could hear her. 'Could you ask her to come out, please? I don't want to disturb her.'

George nodded and spoke into the mic. 'Ellie is with me and she has a message for you.'

'Interview suspended,' Whitney said, leaning in front of Frank to stop the recording.

'Why?' Edwards asked, panic mounting in his eyes.

'We'll be back in a minute.'

Whitney left the room with Frank following. Edwards slumped in his chair, as if all the fight had gone out of him. Did he have an inkling as to why Whitney was leaving the interview?

George went with Ellie into the corridor to join Whitney and Frank.

'Why have you called me out?' Whitney asked Ellie.

'Sorry, guv. Matt asked me to interrupt. The search has turned up photographs of Aimee Edwards and Gavin Curtis together. According to Matt, he'd been following them for quite a while now.'

'Were these photos on a tablet or laptop?' Whitney asked. 'I doubt he'd have physical photos, and I assume he has his phone on him.'

'I'm not sure, guv. Matt didn't say.'

'Thanks for letting me know.' Whitney turned to Frank. 'Let's see what he has to say about this.'

Ellie left them and Whitney and Frank returned to the interview room. Edwards had been studying his hands but looked up as they reappeared.

Whitney switched on the recording equipment. 'Dale, you told us that you had only followed your wife and Gavin Curtis on a few occasions.'

'Yes, that's right,' he said.

'He's lying,' George said to Whitney. 'He's slightly rocking, and his feet are shuffling under the table.'

'Perhaps you can explain, then, why I've heard back from the officers conducting the search at your house saying they've found photographic evidence indicating you've been following your wife and Gavin Curtis for some considerable time.'

Edwards sunk down in his chair and bowed his head. 'I think I need a solicitor,' he muttered.

'That is your prerogative. In the meantime, you'll be escorted to one of the holding cells.'

He clutched at his throat. 'Why can't I wait here?'

'He's panicking,' George said. 'As soon as you mentioned the cell, his whole demeanour changed. You could use it.'

'You are a person of interest in a murder investigation. We have no one available to sit with you and wait until your solicitor arrives. The cells are the only place we can hold you.'

'What about if I cooperate now? Will I be able to go home? I'm claustrophobic. Even the thought of being in a cell is driving me crazy.'

'How does he manage to work under a car then?' George said.

Whitney gave a nod. 'You're a car mechanic. Surely being claustrophobic would prohibit that, especially when you're in the pit.'

'It's different because I work with the garage door open so the fresh air can circulate. I promise, I'm not making this up.'

'Let me confirm, are you going to cooperate with us?' Whitney asked.

'I suppose so,' he muttered, nodding.

'Good. Going back to your previous statement, do you now admit to having followed your wife and her *friend* on many occasions?'

'Yes.'

'Did you ever confront her about it?'

'I'd planned to do so this coming weekend, but then the fire happened. I know it looks bad for me, but I didn't start it. I swear on my daughter's life. Yes, I was there. And, yes, I disappeared once I heard the fire engines. But that was it.'

'What were you doing last Sunday?'

'We visited family in Kettering and arrived back home at around six. We had dinner and watched telly until going to bed at ten.'

'Can anyone vouch for you?' Whitney asked.

'My wife. We were together the whole time,' he said, giving Whitney a questioning gaze, as if unsure why it mattered.

'I believe him,' George said.

'We will be asking your wife to confirm your alibi.'

'Does this mean you're going to tell her I've been following them?' he asked.

'Not necessarily, but I imagine you both have a lot to talk about,' Whitney said.

'I've told you everything I know. May I please leave now?'

'Yes. But we may be in touch again. DC Taylor will show you out.'

Whitney met George in the corridor and waited until Edwards and Frank were out of earshot. 'Well?' she said.

'Don't be disappointed,' George said.

'About what?'

'Having to let him go. I know you'd like to solve this case before the interviews and forthcoming changes, but we don't want to prosecute the wrong person.'

'You're right, of course.' She glanced at her watch. 'Do you have to go back to work, or can you stay a bit longer?'

'Sorry, I do need to go back and collect the work I want to do over the weekend.'

'Do you ever let up? You don't have to work every minute of the day, you know.'

'It suits me. I'm around if you need to speak to me.'

Whitney walked George to the station car park and then went to see Jamieson. As she turned into the corridor to go to his office, he was heading towards her.

'Sir, we need to arrange a press conference.'

'Why? I thought you had someone in custody,' Jamieson said.

'We don't believe the suspect we were holding is responsible for the fires. If possible, I'd like to hold it later this afternoon.'

'I'm not around later. You'll have to hold it by yourself.'

She clamped her mouth shut. What the hell? He'd never allowed her to do a press conference on her own before.

'Okay, sir. I'll arrange it with PR.'

'Good. I can't stop.' He rushed past her and made his way down the corridor, leaving her staring at his retreating back.

Whitney returned to her office and arranged with Melissa for them to hold a press conference at five. That didn't give her much time to call the media in, but she was assured it would be fine.

She'd no sooner ended the call when her phone rang. She glanced at the screen and her heart did a triple flip. It was Martin Finch. Tiffany's dad.

She still found it hard to get her head around them now being friends. She'd spent her entire life telling everyone that the pregnancy had been the result of one drunken night and that the father, who she'd never named, was an utter waste of space. It wasn't a totally accurate description, but it was how she'd chosen to remember it. Yes, they'd both been drunk. But as for him being a *total waste of space,* that couldn't be further from the truth. She'd been so embarrassed after it had happened, that she'd ignored all of his attempts to speak to her. She realised that now, but at the time she'd interpreted the situation in a very different way. Her excuse? She'd only been seventeen at the time.

Whitney had seen Martin several times since they'd met at a recent school reunion and really enjoyed being with him. She had no idea where it was heading, especially as she was in Lenchester and he was in London, but she was happy to let it run. She hadn't mentioned him to her mum. The only person who knew was George, and she wasn't going to be telling anyone. George didn't have a gossiping bone in her body.

'Hello,' she said, finally answering the phone.

'What are you doing?' Martin's soft voice echoed in her ear.

'I'm at work.'

'I wondered if you were around this evening. I've had to go to Birmingham on business and thought I'd come back via Lenchester so we could go out. Any chance?'

'I'm in the middle of an investigation and I've got a press conference at five.'

Why did she say that? Was there still some disconnect between them? She should cut herself some slack. She wasn't working through the night and she'd like to go out with him.

'Oh, well, if you can't, no problem.' She could hear the despondency in his voice.

'Actually, I'd love to. I can't work twenty-four-seven. What time would you like to meet?'

'I'll pick you up from home at seven-thirty. Will that give you enough time?'

The last time they'd been out, she invited him back to her place. She'd planned it in advance and had made sure to tidy up before going out as it had been in its usual messy state, as she rarely had time for any housework. She'd have to leave by six if she was to have any chance of making her house presentable before he came to collect her.

'That would be great. I'll see you later.'

She ended the call and mentally went through her wardrobe deciding what to wear. If he'd been to a business meeting, he was probably going to be dressed fairly smart.

The press conference went well and she was home by six-twenty. She blitzed the house. Granted, it wasn't to George's standard, but it was good enough. After that, she took a shower and got ready. She'd decided to go for a casual pair of black trousers and a wrap-around long sleeved pale blue blouse. At exactly seven-thirty, the doorbell rang. She opened the door and he stood there a bunch of carnations in his hand.

'These are for you,' he said, holding them out.

'Thank you. I can't remember the last time anyone bought me flowers. Come on in while I put them in some water.'

'I've booked us a table at The Post Restaurant. I hope that's all right.'

'Anything's fine if it means I don't have to cook,' she said, laughing.

She scrambled in the cupboard looking for a vase and finally found one that used to belong to her mum. She arranged the flowers and they left the house, climbing into his BMW. What was it about her friends having nice cars when she didn't?

It didn't take long for them to reach the restaurant which was on the outskirts of the city. It wasn't one she'd visited before as it had a reputation for being expensive.

'We were lucky to get a table,' Martin said, as they walked through the double doors. 'I called only minutes after they'd had a cancellation.'

The restaurant was full, and the lighting dimmed. The patrons were wearing a variety of clothes and she didn't feel out of place in what she'd chosen.

The waiter showed them to their table and handed them the menu. There was a white linen tablecloth with matching napkins. A floral centrepiece made with fresh flowers stood in the centre.

'Tell me about this case you're on,' Martin said, after they'd ordered. 'If you can.'

She wouldn't normally discuss work, and it was something she'd drilled into George and the team not to, but it was public knowledge, so she didn't think it would hurt.

'There have been two fires. One is confirmed arson, and we're waiting for the fire officer's report on the second. Fourteen people dead in total.'

'That's dreadful. Let's hope you stop them soon.'

'There's every chance they could have been lit by teenagers

as, according to George, young males set most fires. But the fact that they're setting fire to places with people in them, that's taken it to a whole new level.'

'I'd like to meet George. You talk about her a lot.'

Did she? Whitney smiled to herself. In the grand scheme of things, they hadn't known each other for long, but the woman was already one of the most important people in her life.

'Let's not talk about the fires,' she said, ignoring his request to meet George as she wasn't sure she wanted to do that yet. 'What have you been up to?'

'Boring financial stuff. Not exciting like your life.'

She laughed. 'My life is far from exciting. Chaotic is a better description. Especially as I might not have a job, soon.'

Damn. She hadn't meant to bring up all the crap going on at work.

'Why?' Concern showed in his eyes.

'There's a major restructure going on because of a merger with another force. There aren't enough jobs to go around and we're all being interviewed for our posts.'

'Surely you'll be fine.'

'No one has a *golden pass*, apart from the chief constable. We're all in the same boat. Anyway, let's not talk about work. We're here to enjoy ourselves.'

They spent the rest of the evening talking about everything from their old biology teacher to a psychological thriller they'd watched separately and had both enjoyed. The meal couldn't be faulted and when he pulled up outside her house, she pressed her head against the rich leather car seat, not wanting the evening to end. She invited him in for coffee and was tempted to invite him to stay over, but then changed her mind. She wasn't ready for that. Not yet.

'Are you driving back this evening?' she asked.

'Yes. I have a meeting I can't miss in the morning.'

'On a Saturday?'

'You're not the only one with crazy hours,' he said.

'Agreed. Though, unlike you, I don't seem to spend my entire working life in meetings,' she said, laughing. 'I'd rather be locked in a room full of snakes than that. And I hate snakes more than anything in the world.'

'Yes, meetings do seem to take up an enormous amount of my time. I've had a lovely evening. Hopefully, we can do this again.'

'Yes, that would be nice.'

'Maybe you could come and stay with me in London for a few days, the next time you have some time off.'

A holiday in London with Martin? Butterflies whizzed around her stomach at the thought. In a good way.

'It won't be until the case is over,' she said. 'But, yes. I'd love to.'

FIFTEEN

Monday, 21 September

'Okay, you lot,' Whitney said to the team once they'd all arrived for the day. 'It's been four days since the last fire and we're no closer to finding the culprit or a motive. The fire officer has reported, off the record, that the second fire was arson and carried out in the same manner as the first, and that's as much as we have.' She ran her hands through her hair. Why were they struggling?

'Did you see the death notices of all of the victims from the factory fire in the local paper over the weekend?' Doug asked.

'No. I don't get the paper,' she said.

'I did,' Frank said. 'It brought tears to the wife's eyes. She wondered how the bodies could have been identified if they were so badly burnt.'

'We don't know the extent of burns on the victims, but Aimee Edwards gave the names of people who had attended the rehearsal on Thursday so that would have helped. Also, the pathologists conducting the autopsies would have used dental records if there was no other way of identifying them.'

'That's what I told her,' Frank said.

'Sue, you were following up on leads from Friday's press conference. Has anyone come forward with information that would help?'

She was clutching at straws, as the officer would have mentioned it over the weekend.

'Sorry, guv. There was nothing. A couple of people called in who were at the fire watching, but it turned out that they'd been spoken to on the night.'

'We're going to have to start again, to see if there's anything we've missed.'

'Yes, guv.'

'Ellie, you were looking into Dale Edwards. What did you turn up?'

They might have discounted him, but it didn't hurt to backtrack.

'His finances are a mess. He has an overdraft which is at its limit, and his credit card is maxed out. The household bills are paid by his wife.'

'We know he has a gambling problem, and that he sold his wife's jewellery to pay off his debts. Did you discover any link between him, and Sidney Drake, the owner of the property in the first fire?'

'No, guv.'

'Social media presence?'

'Hardly any. He does have an account but hasn't posted on there for months. And even then, it was a picture of his daughter with their dog.'

'What about the owner of the factory?'

'He's overseas at the moment, guv. I looked into his financials and everything is in order. The director of the theatre group was a friend of his and he allowed them to rehearse there.'

'Okay. Here's what we're going to do. Frank, you and Sue

are to go back over CCTV footage from both fires. Doug, you can revisit everything we have on Sidney Drake. Matt, contact the two students who lived with Cara and Hamish and ask if they can think of anyone who might have set the fire. Ellie, I want you to look again at what you've discovered about Aimee Edwards and Gavin Curtis. We'll have another briefing at five. This case isn't going to get the better of us.'

* * *

At five minutes past seven on Monday evening, George sat in the car, strumming her fingers on the steering wheel, staring at the entrance to the gallery. Should she go in, or should she not? Indecision was a completely alien concept to her. She'd always known what she wanted and went about achieving it.

So why were her palms sweaty and her heart practically beating out of her chest? Had she been wrong to refuse Whitney's offer to accompany her? At the time it had seemed unnecessary, yet here she was plagued by inaction.

She needed to do what she was forever advising Whitney, and what she'd failed to do up to now in this instance. Compartmentalise. She was there to view an exhibition of work, created by a man whose sculptures she admired. Her visit was for artistic reasons only.

And if she believed that, she'd believe anything.

She took one final look in the mirror, smoothed down her hair from where she'd been running her fingers through it, stepped out of the car and strode towards the entrance. There was already a steady flow of people entering the gallery.

If she was honest, she expected to have already seen most of what was on show because each piece took Ross a while to complete, and it hadn't been that long since they'd parted ways. But she was curious to see if he'd completed anything new.

She also wanted to see *him*. It was most confusing. What she wouldn't give for a stiff drink to steady her nerves.

She stood in the doorway and sucked in a breath before marching in. In the centre were a number of podiums each displaying one of Ross's sculptures. She recognised, and loved, several of them, including the life-sized representation of a yellow Labrador puppy held in the arms of a young girl wearing a red skirt, navy jumper, and wellington boots.

People were milling beside the exhibits, and she circled around them, making her way towards the rear of the gallery, deciding to start where it wasn't so packed. As she got closer to the back, her eyes were drawn to a bronze bust.

It was of a woman with an aquiline nose and full mouth, her short hair tucked behind her ears showing off a willowy neck. She did a double take and her mouth dropped open. It was her. Ross had sculptured *her* head and shoulders.

When did he do it? Why did he do it?

He hadn't mentioned anything to her when they were together.

'Do you like it?'

Her heart skipped a beat as she heard the unmistakable soft Irish lilt of Ross's voice in her ear. She turned. He was standing only a couple of feet away, his smile lighting up his blue eyes. And as for his dimples, they'd always got to her. His curly blond hair had grown a little since she'd last seen him, and he appeared to have lost a little weight.

'I was taken aback,' she said, forcing herself to stop gawking. 'I didn't know you'd created it.'

He glanced away for a couple of seconds. Was he embarrassed?

'It was going to be a surprise for you. Then we ... you ...' He paused. 'I'm proud of it so decided to include it in the exhibition.'

'You're selling it?' she challenged. Surely, he wouldn't do

that. Not without her permission. Which she'd never give. She didn't want to be displayed like an object in someone's house.

'No, it's not for sale. Absolutely not. I'm using it as an example of my work in bronze. People like to see what I can do, especially if they're wanting a personal commission.'

She exhaled the breath she'd been holding. Relieved.

'I do like it,' she said, nodding appreciatively. 'Very much.'

'Thank you. I think it's one of the best pieces I've ever done. But with you as a subject it couldn't be anything else. As I've always said, your jawline and symmetrical face are a joy for any artist.'

She shifted awkwardly. She'd always found his compliments difficult to take. She'd never been pretty in the traditional sense of the word. She knew her height and features made a statement and could be intimidating. But whether that made her a good artist's model, she doubted.

'How are you doing, George?' Ross asked, cutting into her thoughts.

'I'm fine, thank you,' she said, giving her usual response.

'What's happened with your father, and the tax evasion charges?'

'Nothing's changed since we last spoke. He's awaiting his trial date, and no one can tell him when that will be, despite him pulling all of the strings he possibly can. I asked Whitney about it and she said it could easily take a year or so. He's back working. His private practice doesn't appear to have been affected. He's still operating on the rich and famous with cardiac issues. In fact, if you saw him you wouldn't realise there was anything amiss. He's acting as if nothing has happened.'

'That sounds like him,' Ross said, laughing.

'He's got himself a good lawyer and that's as much as I know. I haven't spoken to my parents for a while but, as you know, that's not unusual.' She shrugged. It ought to bother her, but she'd learnt to deal with the relationship she had with her parents a long time ago. 'What about you? How are things going?' she asked, anxious to change the topic of conversation.

'I'm extremely busy with work. I have more commissions than I can handle.'

'That's excellent. I'm delighted for you,' she said, meaning it.

She'd been convinced from early on in their relationship that Ross had a great future ahead of him. He worked hard and was gaining recognition. All he needed now was, to quote Whitney, a bit of luck. Not that she believed in luck.

'Are you busy?' Ross asked.

'Always. You know me.'

He'd never complained when she told him she was unavailable to see him because of her workload. It was very different from her previous relationship. Yet, she'd still let Ross go. Whitney's disapproval of her decision, that she'd voiced on many occasions, was still at the forefront of her mind.

'Have you been working with the police recently? Any more serial killers?' he asked, a wry grin on his face.

'We are working on a case. Not, strictly speaking, a serial killer though. We've had two arson attacks recently. Fourteen bodies, so far.'

'That's—'

'Excuse me, Ross.' They both turned at the sound of the voice.

Behind them was an older woman with short grey hair dressed in what she believed to be Vivienne Westwood. Her mother wore the same designer which was why she recognised it.

'George, this is Estelle Norman. She owns the gallery. This is—'

'The woman in your sculpture,' Estelle said, nodding at the bust.

'Yes, that's me. Dr Georgina Cavendish.'

Should she have used her title? It was accepted at work, but was it appropriate at Ross's exhibition?

'I'm sorry to interrupt,' Estelle said. 'I wanted to introduce you to Dina Andreas. She's an art critic with one of the national newspapers. She's promised a good write-up of the exhibition and would like a quote from you.'

'I'll be over in a minute,' Ross said.

Estelle turned and headed towards the centre of the room.

'You're busy. I'll leave you to it and have a look around. It was nice to see you again,' George said, intending to walk away.

'Wait,' Ross said. 'Would you like to go out for a drink after the exhibition?'

Would she? Whitney would tell her to go for it. She wouldn't have come to the gallery if she didn't want to speak to him.

'Yes. That would be nice.'

'Okay.' He looked at his watch. 'We've probably got another hour and a half before people begin to leave. You could—'

'Don't worry about me. I'll bide my time looking at the exhibits and wait for you,' she said, giving a flick of her hand.

'I'd forgotten how self-sufficient you were,' he said, flashing one of his cheeky smiles.

He left her to her own devices, and she moved through the gallery examining each exhibit. Except she wasn't paying close attention because all of the time her head and her heart were having a ping-pong match. The winner to decide on her course of action. Should she stay or should she make a hasty exit? Her heart won.

Finally, after glancing at her watch for what seemed like the hundredth time, the last of the public made their way to the door. Later than she'd anticipated. She'd been positioned at the entrance for the last half an hour and once the gallery was empty, Ross came over.

'Sorry to have kept you waiting. I didn't think it would go on this long.'

'It's not a problem. The exhibition is more important,' she said.

'I'm really hungry. Do you fancy going for something to eat?'

She suspected the only place open for a sit-down meal at this time of night was a fast food burger restaurant. Not her preference.

'How about we grab a takeaway and go back to mine?' she suggested.

His eyes widened. 'Are you sure?'

Why was he so surprised? What had she done wrong? She was only inviting him back for a meal.

'It's easier than having to find somewhere still serving decent food. My place is closer. We can hardly go to yours as it's miles away.'

'Okay. What do you fancy?' he asked.

'You choose,' she said, already knowing the answer.

'How about Thai?' he said.

She smiled to herself. She'd been right. Nine times out of ten it was his takeaway of choice.

'Perfect. I'll go home and warm the plates while you collect it,' she said, taking charge.

Once in the car, she spent the entire journey debating whether she'd done the right thing inviting him back. But she couldn't see why not? They were only having a meal and a catch-up. She, too, hadn't eaten before the exhibition because her stomach had been in knots.

When she arrived home, she warmed the plates and opened a bottle of Pinot Gris from Alsace, its spicy notes of clove and ginger a perfect pairing with Thai food. She'd been saving it for a while. It was one of her favourites. After about twenty minutes, there was a knock at the door. She frowned.

'You didn't have to knock,' she said, as she ushered him in. 'I'd left the door on the latch.'

'I didn't like to, in case you thought I was being a bit presumptuous.'

'Why would I? It's not like you haven't been here before.'

They walked through to the kitchen where she'd set out the plates on the table. She poured them both a glass of wine and they clinked glasses. She took a sip, enjoying the flavour as a warm glow spread over her.

'It's good to see you again, George,' Ross said, peering over the rim of his glass, his cheeks slightly flushed.

'You, too. Your exhibition was fascinating. Although I admit to being a bit perturbed by seeing myself.'

'I'm sorry. Did it upset you?' Worry flashed in his eyes.

'No. It just took me by surprise.'

'Would you like it? It was made for you anyway,' he asked, hesitation in his voice.

Did she want a piece of art with such an uncanny resemblance? She didn't even display photos of herself. Then again, Ross made it. So ... 'Yes, please. I have the perfect spot for it.'

'Don't tell me, in the loo,' he said, laughing.

'No. Why would I put it there?'

'I'm joking, George,' he said, smiling at her.

'Oh.' Heat flooded her cheeks, but the frustration that sometimes accompanied her lack of awareness wasn't there. With Ross she felt safe. 'I was thinking it would look good in the sitting room, above the fireplace.'

'I couldn't think of a better spot. Once the exhibition is finished, I'll bring it over to you,' he said before catching himself. 'Or have it sent ... whichever you prefer?'

'You could bring it yourself,' she suggested.

'I'd like that.' His gaze held hers.

They finished eating and chatting, and it was like it used to be. No awkwardness. She leant back in her chair, the knots in her shoulders fading away as she stared at the fine lines around his eyes. Laughter lines. She'd missed this. Missed him.

She glanced at her watch.

'It's eleven o'clock already.' Where had the time gone?

'I suppose I'd better be going,' Ross said, not actually attempting to move from his spot next to her on the sofa in the sitting room, where they'd gone with their coffee after eating. Disappointment curled up inside of her and she swallowed. Did she want him to leave? She already knew the answer.

'You can stay if you'd like,' she suggested.

'Are you sure?' he said.

'Yes. Or I wouldn't have offered.'

'In the spare bedroom?'

'You know what I mean,' she said, her eyes meeting his. A slow smile spread across his face and he held out his hand. She accepted it and leant forward, her mouth finding his.

SIXTEEN

Tuesday, 22 September

The next morning, George awoke at six. She glanced at Ross fast asleep beside her, the rise and fall of his chest was mesmerising.

She didn't regret it. Why would she? They got on well and were compatible. *Very* compatible. She left the bed without disturbing him, had a shower, and went to the kitchen to make them both a coffee.

Returning upstairs, she met him as he walked out of the bedroom.

'Good morning,' he said, leaning forward to kiss her. She awkwardly held out the coffee tray. He stepped back and studied her, his eyes uncertain.

'Did you sleep well?' she asked, biting down on her bottom lip. Why hadn't she let him kiss her? 'I made coffee.'

'Take it back downstairs and I'll see you after I've had a quick shower. If that's okay?'

'Yes, of course it is.'

Ten minutes later he joined her in the kitchen.

'I really enjoyed myself last night,' he said, as George busied herself wiping down the worktop. She liked having him there, but she also liked having her own space. Especially in the morning.

'As did I,' she admitted.

'George.' Uncertainty flickered in his eyes. 'I'd really like to see you again.'

She swallowed hard. Is that what she wanted? On the one hand, yes. On the other …

'Um …'

'You don't have to make a decision now,' he said softly, the hurt in his voice evident.

'I don't want to cause you further pain. I really enjoyed last night and—' Her phone ringing interrupted her. She glanced at the screen. It was Whitney. It would be something serious as she didn't normally phone so early. 'Sorry, I have to get this,' she said as she picked up the phone from the table.

'There's been another fire,' Whitney said without preamble.

'Whereabouts?'

'It's in a residential area in Thorpeville. 9 Rushmere Close. Can you meet me there?'

'Is it still blazing?'

'I'm not sure. The emergency services were called out at four-thirty this morning.'

'And you've only just been notified?'

'I'm not happy about it, but I'm not going to pursue that at present.'

'Any bodies?'

'I don't know. Can you meet me there?' she repeated, her tone impatient.

'I'll be with you as quickly as I can.'

'Another fire?' Ross asked, as she ended the call.

'Yes. Whitney doesn't know if there are any bodies. I have to leave now. I'll be in touch. Let yourself out.' She grabbed her bag and headed out of the kitchen. She wasn't pleased there was another fire, but she was grateful to have an excuse to leave. To give her time to think.

'Okay. Be careful,' he said.

'I will,' she promised as she hurried down the path to her car. She'd make a decision about him soon.

* * *

Whitney pulled up at the entrance to Rushmere Close, the cul-de-sac in Thorpeville. The morning sun was streaked by thin wisps of black smoke. The houses were all semi-detached and the cordon closed off the entire street. Inside the restricted area were two fire engines and an ambulance. No flames were visible, so she assumed it was now under control. She ducked under the tape and made her way to the fire officer who was standing beside one of the engines. Her nostrils burnt as she breathed in the rancid fumes. He was holding his helmet in his hand. Black smudges covered his face.

'What can you tell me?' she asked, holding out her warrant card for the officer to see.

He shook his head and let out a sigh. 'Three bodies, two children and a woman. They didn't stand a chance. We found them all in their beds. They would have been overcome by the fumes and were asleep so wouldn't have known anything. The fire's now under control, although we've evacuated the rest of the houses in the close as a precaution.'

'Is arson suspected?'

'We won't know officially until our investigator has reported back, but it's similar to the previous two fires. A cloth pushed through the letter box. It looks like we have a serial arsonist on our hands.' He winced.

'Thanks for your input. I'll leave you to it.'

She walked away and looked down the street to see if

George had arrived yet. While waiting she took out her phone and recorded everyone who was watching at the entrance to the close, from behind the cordon. She didn't recognise any of them from the crowd at the factory fire.

As she pocketed her phone, George pulled up. She ducked under the tape and waited while George got out of her car.

'This is dreadful. We've got three bodies. A woman and two children. We haven't identified them yet. I'll have to get Ellie on to it. I've videoed everyone here watching.' She gestured at all the people, huddled in groups, who were peering down the street. 'Do you want to come and take a look?'

'Is it safe?'

'The fire's out, so we should be able to walk around the outside. If you can bear the smell.'

'I've smelled worse,' George said.

They dipped below the cordon and walked down the middle of the road until reaching the house. They stopped and stared at it.

'How many more people have got to die before we can put an end to this?' Whitney shook her head, gripped by the help-lessness which flooded through her.

'Have they confirmed it's the work of the same person?' George asked.

'Not officially, but there are similarities between all three fires.'

'How close can we go to the house?'

'Why, have you spotted something?' Whitney asked, turning to look at George who was staring intently.

'I'm not sure whether it's a trick of the light, but do you see that garden ornament?' She pointed to the grassed area in front of the house where there was a gnome.

'Yes.'

'There's something tied to it.'

'Okay, let's check.'

They headed to the garden and stood a couple of feet away. In front of them was a small garden gnome with a scarf tied around its body. Whitney pulled some disposable gloves from her pocket and an evidence bag. 'I'll take this in case it means anything although it could just be a headscarf that one of the kids used on the gnome.' She photographed the gnome and scarf on the ground and then placed them into the bag. 'Do you want to come back to the station with me?'

'Yes, I have plenty of time,' George said.

They headed back to where they'd parked their cars.

'You're looking very perky this morning. How was the exhibition?' Whitney asked, after noticing the extra spring George had in her step.

'I'll tell you later, when we're at the station.' George closed her car door, ending the conversation. Whitney took a step back as the engine roared to life and George drove away. She blinked. That was abrupt, even by George's standards.

Whatever had happened the previous night had obviously affected her. Whitney couldn't wait to hear more. She would love it if George got back with Ross. They were opposite in so many ways but made the perfect couple. George was more relaxed and less abrasive when she'd been seeing him.

When Whitney made it to the incident room most of the team were already there, including George who was standing by the board.

'Okay, everyone. There's been another fire. George and I have just left the crime scene. There were three bodies, two children and a woman. Ellie, the address is 9 Rushmere Close. Find out who lives there, as we'll need to inform the family.'

'Yes, guv.'

'Was it arson?' Doug asked.

'Unofficially, yes. But we have to wait for the fire service report for final confirmation.'

'Crap,' Doug said. 'Who would do something like that?

That takes the death toll up to seventeen. When we get the bastard, they won't know what's coming to them.'

Whitney swung around to face him. Doug normally took these things in his stride.

'What's got into you?' Frank asked.

'My grandparents died in a fire when I was young,' Doug said, shaking his head.

'Arson?' Frank asked.

'Yes. But they never caught the person responsible.'

'I'm sorry, mate,' Frank said.

'If you'd rather keep off the case, you can.' Why hadn't she known about this before? He'd been on the team for several years.

'No, guv. I want to be here when we nail whoever did it.' Doug thumped the table.

'Okay. But everything is to be done by the book. I videoed all the people who were observing the fire. I can't believe how many people want to stare. Frank, I'll send it to you for comparison with the one from the factory fire. See if there are any similarities.'

'Yes, guv.'

'We found this gnome and scarf in the garden.' She held up the evidence bag and walked over to where Doug was seated. 'Send this to forensics. There might be something that will help with the investigation.'

'Yes, guv.'

'Guv,' Ellie called out. 'The family who lives there is Simon and Hannah Drinkwater with their two children, Lucy and Oscar, aged seven and six.'

'There was no sign of Simon's body, so he must be somewhere else. Find out his details. We'll need to contact him as soon as possible.'

'Yes, guv.'

'Frank, after checking my recordings, I want you to look at

the CCTV footage. It's a residential area, so there might not be much. I want to see if there are any familiar cars, anyone hanging around who'd been at the previous two fires.'

'Will do, guv,' Frank said.

She headed towards George who was standing beside the board, resting one hand on the desk.

'I've got the number for the husband,' Ellie called out, before she'd made it over there.

She turned and hurried to the officer's desk and wrote down the number for Simon Drinkwater.

'Thanks. I'll give him a call as we don't know where he is.'

She headed straight for her office, leaving George in the incident room with the others. She'd rather deliver the news on her own. It was hard enough to do face to face, but it was even worse when it had to be done on the phone, as it was difficult to gauge the impact of the words on the recipient and act accordingly.

'Is this Simon Drinkwater?' she asked, once the phone had been answered by a male who didn't state his name.

'Yes. Who is this?'

'Detective Chief Inspector Walker from Lenchester CID. Could you tell me where you are at the moment?'

'I'm in London. Why do you want to know? Has something happened?' he said, his voice louder and higher pitched.

Whitney sucked in a breath. 'I'm very sorry to have to inform you, there's been a fire at your home in Rushmere Close.'

'A fire? What happened? Are my wife and children okay? Tell me they're fine. A fire. I don't believe it.' The words tumbled from his mouth. 'What—'

'Mr Drinkwater,' she said gently, pausing for a few seconds to ensure he'd stopped talking. 'I'm so sorry. Unfortunately, there were no survivors.'

'Oh my God,' he said, letting out a low moan.

'We have yet to identify the people who were in the house. But we do believe it's your wife and two children. Hannah, Lucy, and Oscar.'

The ominous silence echoed in Whitney's ears.

'When was the fire?' he finally asked, his voice barely above a whisper.

'It started during the night, I'm not sure of the exact time. We're waiting for the fire service report to confirm the cause. Are you able to come home straight away? I could send someone to collect you.' She didn't think driving after having been given such news was a good idea.

'I was due to be coming back today, by train.'

'Would you like me to arrange for you to be collected and brought back to Lenchester?' she repeated the offer.

'Thank you. Yes.'

'I'm very sorry for your loss. Someone will be in touch shortly to make the arrangements. Please wait for their call before doing anything.'

'I can't believe this has happened. Are you sure it's them?' A sob escaped his lips. 'Sorry,' he muttered.

'Please don't apologise,' she said, her words sounding empty and trite. The man had just had his life destroyed. 'We will need you to make a formal identification, until we can confirm, but we do believe so.'

She ended the call and stayed in her office for a few minutes, taking deep breaths until her heart rate returned to normal. She hated feeling so helpless.

* * *

Two hours later, while Whitney and her team were studying shots of the latest fire, a phone on the main incident room desk rang. She went over and answered it.

'Walker.'

'Mr Drinkwater has arrived,' the officer on the front desk said.

'We'll be down in a minute. Give him a cup of tea and settle him into one of the interview rooms.'

'Yes, guv.'

'George, Simon Drinkwater is here. You can come with me and we'll see if he knows anything which might help us.'

'Okay,' George said.

When they arrived, Simon Drinkwater was seated behind a table, with a mug of tea in front of him. His face was devoid of colour and his eyes were bloodshot. He was a well-built man, with cropped dark brown hair, dressed in a navy suit, and a white open-necked shirt. His office attire was at odds with the helpless expression on his face.

'Mr Drinkwater. I'm Detective Chief Inspector Walker, we spoke earlier. This is Dr Cavendish. Do you feel up to answering a few questions?'

'Yes. When can I go home? I know I can't live there, but I want to see it for myself. To see what happened.'

'I'm very sorry, but you won't be allowed on the site for a while as it's cordoned off until it's safe and the investigation into the fire has been completed. Do you have anywhere you can stay?'

'I'll book into a hotel.'

'Are any of your family close by?' It wasn't wise for him to be alone at a time like this.

'No. Both of our families live in Norfolk.' He swallowed. 'I'll have to contact them and let them know what's happened.'

'Any friends?'

'I want to be on my own.'

'I understand,' she said gently. 'When was the last time you were in contact with your wife?'

'Yesterday. I spoke to her and the children before they went out for dinner. Hannah took them out for a pizza as a special treat.'

'What time was this?'

'Around five-thirty, I think. Hannah texted me at eight to say they were home, and she was getting them ready for bed.'

'Can you tell me what you were doing in London?'

'I was there on business.'

'What do you do?'

'I'm a sales consultant for a global exhibition and conference company. Our head office is in Chiswick and we were having training for a new product that's being launched next month. It's easier for me to stay in London than travel back and forth each day.'

'Why didn't you come home last night, after the training had finished?' Whitney asked.

He glanced away. 'Because we were going out for a meal afterwards and I wanted to be able to drink.'

What was he hiding?

'Doesn't that waste a day? If you'd come home last night …' She paused. He might have been dead if he had.

'Are you sure you can't tell me anything about how the fire started?' he asked, not appearing to register what she'd just said.

She would tell him, before the media did.

'We have a strong suspicion that it's arson. This is the third fire we've had recently in the area and we believe they might all be linked.'

His dark eyes widened. 'Were they murdered?'

'Can you think of anybody who might have a grievance against you and your family?'

'No, of course not. They were two innocent children, for God's sake. That would be ridiculous. The same as my wife. No one would.' Tears formed in his eyes and he brushed them away with the back of his hand.

Whitney reached for the box of tissues at the end of the

desk and placed them in front of him. He took one out and wiped his eyes.

'Is there anyone who might want to get to *you*?' Whitney asked.

'No. What sort of person do you think I am? We're ordinary people. With ordinary jobs and ordinary lives. And if this is one of several fires, how can it be something to do with any single person in one of the places?'

'To put us off discovering the real motive. We do have to examine every eventuality. You said you were in London last night. Where did you stay?'

'I was at the Harvest Hotel, in Kensington.'

'Is there anyone who can vouch for you?'

'You can check with the hotel,' he said, not able to meet her eyes.

She'd speak to George about that. Something wasn't quite right. It was the second time he'd avoided looking directly at her when she'd asked a straightforward question. Unless he wasn't where he'd said he was.

'We will, thank you. If you could let us know where you're going to be staying, once you know, we'll be in contact to arrange the formal identification.'

They escorted him back to the front of the station and waited until he'd left the building.

'He was hiding something,' George said, as they were on their way back to the incident room.

'Yes, I noticed, too.'

'I suspect he either wasn't where he said he was, or he was doing something he shouldn't.'

'Either way, it needs investigating. I'll get one of the team on to it when we get back.'

'I'm going to the university, if you don't need me,' George said.

'Okay. I'll walk you to your car, as I want you to tell me how it went last night at the exhibition. Did you get to spend much time with Ross?'

'It was very interesting,' George said, avoiding looking at her as they made their way to the door at the rear of the station.

'Bloody hell, not you, too,' Whitney groaned.

'I don't understand,' George said, coming to a standstill.

'You understand perfectly. You're doing the same as Drinkwater, not meeting my eyes. Now tell me the truth. What happened last night?'

'I'm not avoiding telling you anything. I had an enjoyable time. When you phoned this morning, it was just after Ross had asked me if we could see each other again.'

'He got in touch at six-thirty in the morning? How did he know you were ... Ohhhhh—' Whitney broke off and grinned. Go, George. 'I get it. He stayed the night. No point in denying it.'

'I wasn't going to,' George said, this time not breaking eye contact.

'And?'

'I don't understand,' George said.

'Stop with the *not understanding*. I can spell it out if you wish. Are you going to go back out with him?'

'I haven't decided. It's highly likely.'

'I knew there was something different about you this morning. You had an extra spring in your step. You can't hide this stuff from me.' She gave a smug smile.

'You were imagining things. We met at the fire, and I'm sure I wasn't bouncing when I walked.'

'You have it your way,' Whitney said, shrugging. 'I know what I saw. Anyway, what did you actually tell him when he asked?'

'I didn't have time to answer as you phoned, and I had to leave.'

'And because Ross is such a great guy, he understood and is

prepared to wait for you to make up your mind. You seriously don't know how lucky you are having a guy like him.'

'I'll give the matter some thought and get back to him. He did give me a present. Although I haven't yet received it.'

'Tell me.'

'At the exhibition there was a bronze bust on display, of me. He said he'd made it as a surprise but then we broke up. He asked if I would like it.'

'Wow. He loves you so much that he made a statue of you. Seriously, George, don't let him go again. Because if you do, I might be tempted to pursue him myself.'

'You want a relationship with Ross?' George asked, glaring at her.

'Look at you. I'm only joking. But it proves one thing. Whatever you might say, you have strong feelings for him.'

'I admit, there is something between us.'

'So, you're going to say yes to going back out with him?' Whitney asked, as they reached George's car.

'I'm going to think about it.'

'You drive me crazy, do you know that? We'll finish this conversation another time.'

SEVENTEEN

Tuesday, 22 September

Whitney walked into the incident room and headed towards the board where she wrote the name of the husband, and London next to it.

'Attention, everyone,' she called out, waiting for the chatter to stop. 'We've just spoken to the husband and father of the latest victims. He was away on business at the time of the fire.'

'That's suspicious,' Frank said.

'We'll check his alibi. Sue, you can do that. He stayed at the Harvest Hotel in Kensington. Find out when he checked in and out. Also, we want to know whether he paid using cash or credit card. He said it was a business trip. If it was, it's unlikely he would have paid by cash.' She wasn't sure why she believed that was important. A hunch, maybe.

'Yes, guv,' Sue said.

'Frank, did you get anything from the videos I recorded on my phone?'

'The people you captured were different on both days, but I did notice that one of the paramedics was the same.'

'Contact the ambulance service and find out the names of the crew members for both fires. It may be nothing but, as we all know, sometimes it's first responders who set fires for a variety of reasons, of which I'm sure George would be able to tell us.'

'Yes, guv.'

'I'm expecting a member of the fire service to come in shortly to discuss their findings following the investigations of the first two fires. We already know they suspect arson.' Her phone rang. 'This might be them.'

'Fire Investigation Officer Osborne is here to see you, guv,' the desk sergeant said.

'I'll be down shortly.'

When she arrived downstairs, the officer was seated close to the front desk.

'Fire Investigation Officer Osborne?'

'Call me Roger,' the older officer said.

'I'm Detective Chief Inspector Walker. Whitney. Thank you for coming in.'

'I wanted to go through my report with you, rather than waiting for it to reach you through the usual channels.'

'I appreciate it as, at the moment, we don't have any suspects. Anything you can tell me that might help the investigation, I'd be extremely grateful for.'

She took him into one of the interview rooms, stopping on the way for a coffee for them both.

'The first fire was set deliberately. The source was at the front door, and there was evidence of an accelerant-coated rag pushed through the letter box onto the floor. There were two cigarette butts located on the floor close by and we suspect when lit they were pushed through the letter box. The fire immediately took hold, going up the stairs to where the victims were asleep in their bed.'

Her body tensed. 'What arsewipe would do that?' She paused as a niggling thought came to the front of her mind.

'Wouldn't the butts have been burnt away if they were at the starting point of the fire?'

'You'd think so, but often butts can survive a fire.'

'What can you tell me about the second fire?'

'An accelerant-soaked cloth was pushed through the factory letter box. Cigarette butts found close by, inside the building.'

'Two butts again?'

'Yes.'

'Where are these butts?' There could be some forensics on them.

'SOCO took them. I don't know whether anything useful could be obtained.'

'Do you believe we have two arsonists working together?'

'It's possible. Unless it was a single person wanting to make sure the fire took hold by using two cigarettes.'

If the fires were set by a young male, as George had suggested, it would be entirely possible that there were two working together. Teens liked to hang around in pairs, or groups.

'The front door had been locked by the theatre director, to prevent kids from coming in. How come no one could get out of the side entrance they used?'

'From what we could establish, apart from the two people who were rescued, the group were all in the main factory area. There was a room close by, most likely a maintenance store, which contained a variety of solvents, including cleaners for machine parts, and insecticides. These acted as further incendiaries. The fire would have taken hold in there first and then blocked the way out of the main area where the victims were rehearsing.'

'Were the victims burnt alive?' She winced.

'Smoke and fume inhalation would have rendered them unconscious before the flames got to them, although most of the bodies were recognisable as the fire officers were able to put out the fire quickly,' Roger said.

'Were there no fire doors?'

'Not in the open area where they were rehearsing,' Roger said. 'From our investigation, we believe the two who survived did so because they were unable to open the door between the offices leading to the factory area.'

'Was *that* a fire door?' Whitney asked.

'Yes, but it was a wooden one, not up to the latest specification, and it had rotted in places, which is why smoke was able to penetrate underneath and cause them respiratory difficulties. Luckily, they were rescued before they died.'

'How come the door was rotten? Don't buildings like that have regular fire inspections?'

'It was no longer a factory, and the permission given to the theatre group wasn't official. It was done as a favour.'

'Some *favour*.' She shook her head. 'Do your findings indicate that the same person who committed the first fire, was also responsible for the second?'

'Yes, we believe both were committed by the same person. There are too many similarities.'

'We've now got a third fire and I was told by one of your officers, unofficially, that it was similar to the first two. How quickly before we can have your report?'

'We'll work as quickly as possible, but there are protocols to follow, as I'm sure you're aware.'

'I understand. Thank you for taking the time to come in.'

She showed the officer out of the station and returned to the incident room.

'Listen up, everyone. It has been confirmed that the first two fires were arson and, according to the report, most likely carried out by the same person, or persons.'

'Do they believe there was more than one person involved?' Matt asked.

'It's possible, because two cigarette butts were found close to the origin of both fires.'

'What about the third?'

'We have to wait for the official report but, for the moment, we're going to assume it, too, was arson. I need to see Jamieson to arrange another press conference. People need to be extra vigilant.'

She went upstairs to Jamieson's office and knocked on his door. It looked as though he was on his way out as he was doing up the silver buttons on his uniform jacket.

'Hello, sir.'

'What is it, Walker?'

'I've just come to let you know where we are. The first two fires have been confirmed as arson, possibly by the same person or persons. There's been a third fire, which you may or may not know about. This time there were no survivors. The victims were a woman and her two children.'

'Oh, my goodness.'

'Arson isn't confirmed, but for the moment we're treating it as such. We need to arrange a press conference as soon as possible.'

'I'm on my way out to a meeting now. I'll ask my assistant to arrange with PR to hold one this afternoon.'

'Around two o'clock would be good,' she said.

'Leave it with me and I'll let you know. I've got to go,' he said, dismissing her with a flick of his hand.

'Yes, sir.' She left and went back down to the incident room.

* * *

Whitney hurried down to the press conference room to meet Jamieson. She was late. The care home where her mother lived had called, wanting to arrange a time when she could take her mum out for lunch. They liked to plan in advance when possible. Whitney would phone the home where her brother was to arrange for him to join them. It had been a while since the three of them spent some time together, because Whitney had been so busy at work. But that was no excuse. She needed to make more of an effort. Her mum's dementia was getting worse, and soon she might not recognise Whitney and her brother. They needed to make the most of the time they had left.

When she arrived, Jamieson was standing with his arms tightly folded across his chest, tapping his foot.

'Sorry I'm late, sir. I got caught on the phone.'

'Yes, that's what you always say.'

She thought he hadn't realised that was her go-to excuse. Ironic that this time it was true.

'It's busy,' she said, trying to make light of it.

'Come on. I've got other things to do besides this,' he said.

He could have left her to do it, as he had previously, if he was that busy. Although it wouldn't look good to his superior officers if he missed another one.

Melissa opened the door and they walked in. As usual, the room was packed. Cameras at the back, hanging over the reporters who were sitting in the front rows. As they walked in and sat down, everyone stopped talking.

'Thank you for coming in to see us,' Melissa said. 'I'll hand you over to Detective Superintendent Jamieson.'

'Good afternoon. We've called you in to let you know that there's been another fire. We believe this too is arson, although we're awaiting confirmation from the fire service. This latest fire took place in Rushmere Close, in the early hours of the morning. We would like to speak to anyone who was in the area at the time. All calls will be kept confidential.'

'How many victims?' one of the reporters called out.

'I'll hand you over to Detective Chief Inspector Walker and she'll fill you in on the details.'

He slid the microphone over to Whitney. 'There were three

victims in this latest fire. A woman and two children aged six and seven. A boy and a girl.'

A hush went over the room, as it always did whenever children were harmed.

'Can you tell us their names?' a reporter in the front row asked.

'No, we're not releasing names at present.' Although it wouldn't take long for them to find out who the victims were, once they knew the exact location of the fire. 'But I'd like to reiterate what Detective Superintendent Jamieson said. We'd like anyone who was in the area at the time to contact us. Also, we would like to hear from any person who believes they have information about these arson attacks.'

'How many victims in total do we have from the fires?' another reporter asked.

'Seventeen,' Whitney said.

'Do you have any suspects?'

'We're not able to discuss the details of our investigation, other than to say that the fire service has confirmed arson regarding the first two fires.'

She ended the conference and left with Jamieson. They walked in silence down the corridor.

'Let's hope we get a lead from this,' she said.

'Yes. We can do without further fires. Have you been given your interview date yet, Walker?'

His question took her by surprise. Didn't he know? She thought he'd have been kept informed.

'Yes. It's on Thursday. What about you?' she asked.

'Mine's coming up, too. Make sure you're well-prepared. There's a lot of competition,' he said staring at her.

'Yes, sir, I will.'

'If you want to carry on in your current role, it's imperative to be ready because you're up against people from both stations.'

'Yes, sir, I will be. Thank you.'

They reached the end of the corridor and parted ways. She continued to the incident room. Was he helping her? Did he actually want her to get the job? She'd assumed he didn't care one way or the other, but maybe she'd misjudged him. On her part, she was hoping that he didn't get his. Then again, was it better the devil you know?

EIGHTEEN

Wednesday, 23 September

Whitney arrived at work early, intending to go straight to her office and do some preparation for her interview. She didn't want to lose her job and being moved to another station was out of the question because of her mum and brother. They might both be in care homes, but that didn't mean she could relinquish her responsibility towards them. They both needed her. She was the link between them. Neither of them would understand if the visits had to stop because Whitney moved and couldn't make it happen.

It wasn't even a decision. If they offered her a position somewhere else, in another county, she'd resign. No question. But where would that leave her? If she wasn't in the force, her options were slim.

'Guv,' Matt called out as she'd almost reached her office door. She turned.

'Yes?'

'We might have something.'

She rushed over to his desk, thoughts of her interview pushed to the back of her mind. 'What?'

'Scarlett Bryant, a friend of Hannah Drinkwater, is downstairs. She told Dave on the front desk that she had important information about the couple.'

Whitney's skin prickled, as it always did when an investigation took a turn for the better. George had been convinced Simon Drinkwater was hiding something, were they about to find out what it was?

'Did Dave say anything else?' Whitney asked.

'No. Do you want to come with me to speak to her, or shall I go on my own?' Matt asked, as he pushed back his chair and stood.

'We'll go together.'

They headed downstairs to the interview room where the woman was sitting. She was in her thirties and casually dressed in jeans and a grey V-neck jumper. Her short dark hair was tucked behind her ears, revealing some small diamond studs. Her hands were clenched into fists and rested on the table. Her face was pale, and her eyes puffy.

'Hello, Scarlett. I'm Detective Chief Inspector Walker and this is Detective Sergeant Price,' Whitney said, gently to put the woman at ease. 'I understand you'd like to talk to us about Hannah and Simon Drinkwater.'

There was silence for a few seconds.

'I had to come forward and tell you what I know,' Scarlett finally said, her voice quiet.

'Do you mind if I record this?' Whitney asked, as she went to lean over and press the button.

Worried eyes stared back at her. 'Do you have to? I'd rather you didn't if that's allowed.'

'We only record interviews to save taking notes. It's not a problem for me not to,' she reassured her.

'Thank you.' Scarlett exhaled a loud breath.

She was scared. That much was obvious. What on earth was going on?

Whitney pulled out her notebook and pen and began scribbling.

'What's your full name and address?' Whitney asked.

'Scarlett Ebony Bryant and I live at 26 Hinton Street, in Bidwell.'

Whitney knew the village. It was about five miles out of Lenchester.

'You were Hannah's friend, I believe.'

'Yes. We met at school and were best friends for years. I can't believe what's happened to them. They were lovely children.' Tears formed in her eyes and she blinked them away.

'What is it you wanted to tell us?' Whitney asked.

'Have you met Simon?' she asked, biting down on her bottom lip.

'Yes, we've met Mr Drinkwater.'

'Don't you think it was strange that he wasn't there at the time of the fire?' She leant forward and stared directly at Whitney. Now they were getting somewhere. She clearly had an issue with the husband.

'He was away on business and we are currently verifying his alibi.'

Scarlett swallowed. 'Did you talk to him about his marriage?'

Whitney exchanged a glance with Matt. He, too, leant forward slightly.

'Could you be more explicit?' Whitney asked.

'Hannah and Simon were together for many years. He was the perfect partner before they got married. Almost too perfect. Not that I said anything to her as she was so besotted with him.'

'You don't like him?' Whitney asked.

'At first, I did, but there was something about him that unnerved me. I couldn't put my finger on it, though.'

'Did you mention this to anyone?'

'No. I kept it to myself because he seemed so popular with everyone.'

'What is it you want us to know?' Whitney asked, wondering whether this was going to be of use. She couldn't afford the time to sit around hoping for a solid lead. She needed to go back to her office and prepare for Thursday.

'After Hannah had Lucy, her eldest, he changed.'

'In what way?' Whitney asked.

'He became abusive both physically and emotionally.'

The words hung in the air and Whitney swallowed. Her hunch had been right, but she almost wished it hadn't been. Domestic abuse cases were always so heartbreaking.

'Did she report it to the police?' Matt asked.

'No, she wouldn't, even though I begged her to. She was scared.'

'We would have offered her protection,' Matt said.

'You don't know what he was like. He was careful to make sure no one knew. Hannah didn't even mention it to me until I saw some bruising and made her tell me. She was relieved to share it with someone. Once I knew, she would speak openly about it. I offered to help her escape and at one time I thought she was going to. But she backed out at the last minute, saying that she couldn't do it to the children because they loved their father.'

'Did Oscar and Lucy have any idea about what was happening?' Whitney asked.

'I don't think so. They were young and went to bed early. He was at his worst then. Why didn't I try harder to persuade her to leave? She might still be alive if I'd insisted.' She banged her hand on the table, anguish in her eyes.

'Did he know you were aware of what was happening?'

'I'm not sure. If he was, he didn't say anything to me or Hannah. Whenever anyone was there, he acted as if he was totally in love with her but as soon as they were on their own, if she'd ever stepped out of line, he was extremely nasty to her.'

'Did you witness any of this behaviour?' At the moment, they only had Scarlett's word for it. There could be any number of reasons why she would want the police to believe it.

'Just the once. I was visiting and had gone to the loo. Simon didn't realise I was there. I heard him shouting at her for being lazy and not having dinner prepared. As soon as I walked into the kitchen, he stopped and laughed, pretending he was joking. I can still see the fear in her eyes.'

'Where were the children?' Whitney asked, as previously everything had been kept away from them.

'They were playing upstairs in their bedrooms with the doors shut. They wouldn't have heard.' She let out a groan. 'Why didn't I do something? This all could have been prevented.'

'We don't know that,' Whitney said. 'We have no evidence that Mr Drinkwater caused the fire. It's one of several we're investigating.'

'Even if he didn't, had she moved then she wouldn't have been in the house when the fire was set. She'd have been somewhere else with the children.'

'Try not to blame yourself. Is there anything else we should know?' Whitney asked.

Scarlett paused for a moment. 'Yes. Hannah suspected Simon of having an affair.'

Interesting. Was he with the woman on the night in question? That would certainly account for his evasiveness when being interviewed.

'How did she know?'

'She saw some texts on his phone, and there were some mysterious purchases on his credit card. She looked at the statements when he was out one time.'

'How did she feel about this affair? Was she hoping he would leave her for this other woman?'

She shook her head. 'This is what I didn't understand. She didn't want him to leave them. It was the only thing that Hannah and I had ever disagreed over. I told her she'd be better off without him, but she said she couldn't manage on her own. It made no sense. I offered her somewhere to stay and some money to tide her over, but she refused.'

If Scarlett had seen some of the things Whitney had, over the years, it would make total sense. But she wasn't going to explain that. They needed to move forward on investigating Simon Drinkwater.

'We'll investigate further, thank you for coming in to see us.'

'Please don't mention you heard this from me as I don't trust him to not come after me.'

'Our conversation is confidential. We won't bring you into it,' Whitney said.

'Thank you. I hope it wasn't him. But knowing what he's like … well …'

Whitney and Matt escorted Scarlett to the station entrance and then returned to the incident room. She walked to the board and made a note against Simon Drinkwater's name.

'We've just interviewed a friend of Hannah Drinkwater,' she said to the team. 'It seems that the husband isn't as loving and caring as he made out when interviewed. According to the friend, Drinkwater was abusive towards his wife and it's believed that he was having an affair.'

'Not another affair,' Frank said. 'You do realise this is the third one we've come across in this case. First Newman, then the survivors of the theatre fire, and now Drinkwater.'

'It's just a coincidence,' Whitney said.

'You know what Dr Cavendish would say about that,' Frank said.

'I do. But this time she's wrong. We need Drinkwater back

here pronto. He told us he'd be staying at a hotel. Matt, you get onto that,' she said looking at her officer.

'Will do, guv,' Matt said.

'Do you think he might have started all the fires?' Frank asked.

'We don't know, but this line of enquiry certainly needs pursuing. Ellie, I want you to investigate him. Friends. Family. Finances. Work. A possible mistress. Anything on him you can get.'

'Yes, guv.'

Whitney pulled out her phone and hit speed dial.

'Hello, Whitney.' George answered on the second ring.

'Any chance you can come to the station?'

'Yes. Do you have a new lead?' George asked.

'According to a source, Simon Drinkwater not only physically and emotionally abused his wife but was also having an affair.'

'I expect he was with her in London. It would certainly explain his behaviour when we interviewed him,' George said.

'That's exactly what I thought. Whether he's involved in the arson attacks remains to be seen, but we certainly need to speak to him again to find out exactly where he was and what he'd been doing. I'd like you here to observe his interview.'

'What time do you need me?'

'Hold on a moment. I'll find out. Matt,' she called out. 'Did you get hold of Drinkwater?'

'Yes, guv. He's coming in straight away.'

'What did you tell him?'

'That we needed some more details.'

'George,' she said, holding the phone back to her ear. 'Come in as soon as possible. He's going to be here shortly.'

Whitney ended the call and went to her office. She had a few minutes to spare, so she could actually start on the preparation for tomorrow's interview. She'd only got a little way in when Matt knocked and walked in.

'Simon Drinkwater has arrived.'

'Arrange for him to be put into one of the interview rooms and we'll go down as soon as George arrives. Hold that thought,' she added as George walked through the incident room towards them.

'He's here already,' she said when the psychologist got closer. 'Matt and I will interview him, and you can observe from outside.'

'There's a surprise,' George said, arching an eyebrow.

Whitney grinned, enjoying her friend cracking a joke which she didn't do often.

When they reached the interview room, George went into the connecting room to observe and Matt and Whitney walked in.

'Hello, Mr Drinkwater. Thank you for coming back in to see us,' Whitney said, relaxing her voice so as not to alert him.

'If I can help in any way. I want to get the bastard who's totally destroyed my life. I'll ...' His voice broke.

'He appears genuine,' George said. 'Nothing so far to indicate he's not telling the truth. Though you've only just begun.'

'I'm going to record the interview,' Whitney said, pressing the recording equipment. 'Interview, twenty-third of September. Those present: Detective Chief Inspector Walker, Detective Sergeant Price. Please state your name,' she said to Drinkwater.

'Simon Drinkwater. Is it necessary to record our conversation?' he asked, frowning.

'It's easier than taking notes,' Whitney said, trotting out her usual answer. 'We would like to speak to you about your relationship with your wife.'

'My relationship? Why?'

'It's usual in these investigations. We have to cover all lines of enquiry.'

'Hannah and I had a great relationship. Everything was fine between us.'

'He didn't blink once when telling you that. You know what that means,' George said in her ear.

She gave a tiny nod.

'That's not what we've been led to believe.'

He scowled at her. 'I don't know what you mean. My wife's dead so why are you asking me these questions? It's an insult to her memory.'

'Is it right that you were often physical towards your wife?'

He glanced away. 'Absolutely not.'

'He's lying,' George said in her ear. 'Push harder.'

'We've been informed that you were both physically and emotionally abusive towards Hannah and that it started after the birth of your first child.'

His eyes darted from Whitney to Matt. Did he think the officer would side with him?

'Let me guess. Scarlett-fucking-Bryant fed you that gossip. She's never liked me. She was jealous because I took Hannah away from her. There was one time when she heard me lose my temper and then concluded that I beat my wife up. I object to being accused in this way.'

'Mr Drinkwater, all we want is the truth,' Whitney said, her voice flat.

'So do I. I know your game. You're trying to pin the fire on me, but I was in London, as I've already told you, and it can be verified.'

'Who were you with at the hotel in London?' Was he going to admit to having the affair Scarlett had accused him of?

'I was alone.'

'Another lie,' George said. 'Look at the way he blinked furiously after speaking. This man is a textbook case.'

Whitney suppressed the urge to smile at George's comment.

'If you don't tell us the truth, we will charge you with obstruction of justice.' She locked eyes with him, but he couldn't maintain contact.

'I'm not obstructing anything.'

'Have you been seeing someone else recently?' He coloured slightly and remained silent. 'Mr Drinkwater, please answer the question.'

'Yes, I have,' he muttered.

Finally, they were getting somewhere. Not that it was helping to solve the fires, but at least he was telling the truth.

'Who is this person?' she asked.

'A woman I met at a conference earlier in the year.' His shoulders slumped.

'Were you with her on the night of the fire?'

He finally looked up at her. 'Yes.'

'Now he's telling the truth,' George said.

'I want the name of this person so she can verify where you were.' Whitney took out her pad and pen from her pocket and slid it across the table.

'I don't want her involved. I was in London, attending training. I can show you my diary.'

'But that doesn't mean you didn't come back at some time during the night to set the fire.' She didn't think it was possible, but she wasn't going to let him off that easily.

'Why would I set fire to our house knowing my children were in there? I'd never do that. Never.' A single tear rolled down his cheek.

'Mr Drinkwater, I want the name and contact details of the woman you were with.'

He picked up Whitney's pen and, after writing it all down, pushed the notebook towards her. 'Here you are,' he muttered.

Whitney glanced at it. *Charlotte Payne*. She lived in Rugby, not far away. He said he'd be staying at a hotel now his house was inhabitable. Was he? Or was he with her?

'Was Charlotte with you the whole time while you were in London?'

'Yes. She took leave this week and came with me.'

'Where does she work?'

'She's a PR assistant for a company in Rugby.'

'Are you staying in Rugby with her now?'

'Yes,' he said, bowing his head.

'Is she at home at the moment?'

'No. She's waiting in the car park for me. I couldn't face driving.'

'What car does she drive?'

'A red Vauxhall Corsa. She parked in the top right corner.'

She turned to Matt. 'Ask someone to bring Charlotte Payne into the station and put her in one of the interview rooms.'

'Yes, guv,' Matt said, as he got up and left.

'Interview suspended.' Whitney leant across and stopped the recording.

'I can't believe that you thought I would do anything to harm my family,' Simon Drinkwater said.

'It's nothing personal. Once we'd been informed that your relationship wasn't as good as you'd told us, we were duty-bound to investigate.'

Was he going to admit to being abusive now the recording had been turned off?

'Occasionally, things did get out of hand in our relationship, and I acted badly. I'm not proud of myself but I would never have done anything to harm my children. Never. You have to believe me.'

'You can stay here while we speak to Charlotte,' Whitney said, coldly.

'You still think I did it?'

She ignored his question and left the interview room, going next door to see George.

'A nasty piece of work.' She shuddered.

'He's lost his entire family,' George said. 'He'll be suffering.'

'A person less kind than me would say he deserved to suffer after his behaviour. Let's speak to the woman he was with as I've got a nagging feeling there's more to this than we know.'

'Nagging feelings are hardly scientific,' George said, shaking her head.

'Thank you, *Miss Logical,* for your input, but you'll see that I'm right.'

NINETEEN

Wednesday, 23 September

George followed Whitney as she strode to the other interview room where Charlotte Payne was waiting. Her friend needed to put aside her feelings for Drinkwater if she was to be level-headed in the interview.

'Do you want me to observe?' she asked, as they were on their way.

'No. You can come in with me. It shouldn't take long.'

They walked in and seated was an attractive woman with wavy dark hair which came to her shoulders, the type seen in TV commercials for shampoo. Her clothes were clearly expensive and when they entered the room, she glanced up and smiled at them. But it didn't quite reach up to her hazel eyes.

Her manner put George on alert.

'Thank you for coming in. I'm Detective Chief Inspector Walker and this is Dr Cavendish. We'd like to speak to you about Simon Drinkwater.'

'Happy to help,' Charlotte said, as she tapped her dark pink manicured nails on the table.

It was all too staged for George's liking.

'Tell us about being in London with Simon,' Whitney said.

'We were together apart from when he was in training, during which time I went shopping. On Monday evening we took in a show and then went back to the Harvest Hotel where we were staying.'

She was sure Whitney's team would be able to track that. Theatre tickets would have been paid using a card, she imagined.

'How long have you been seeing Simon?' Whitney asked.

'A little over six months.'

'Even though he's married.'

'What's that got to do with anything?' She scowled, for a moment dropping the façade, but almost immediately returning to how she'd been.

George gently nudged Whitney with her foot under the table. This wasn't the time for her to pass comment on the affair. It was the one thing that always got to Whitney. George hadn't asked why. Maybe Whitney's father had had an affair. Though from how Whitney had described her parents' relationship, she doubted it.

'Where did you meet?' Whitney asked.

'In Birmingham at a conference on PR strategy in a global environment.'

'How often do you and Simon see each other?' Whitney asked.

'It depends. Whenever he goes away on business, I'll accompany him, providing I can get the time off work.'

'You live in Rugby, I believe,' Whitney said. 'But you don't come from this area, judging by your accent.'

'I'm originally from Bristol, further south.'

'Simon is staying with you at the moment. Do you envisage it will be permanent?' George asked, knowing Whitney wouldn't like her asking questions, but she wanted to delve deeper into the relationship.

'I hope so.' She smiled again. 'We're in love. What happened to his family was awful but the one thing that came out of it is that we can now be together and don't have to hide our relationship.'

No sign of remorse shown towards the death of the wife and children. Had she been involved in the fire?

George glanced at Whitney, whose face was set hard.

'During the time you and Simon have been together, have you had any fights?' Whitney asked.

'Fights?'

'Any arguments or disagreements?' Whitney asked.

'No. We get on very well. He's excellent company. The perfect partner.'

'He hasn't been physical with you at all?' Whitney asked.

Charlotte stared at them, confusion in her eyes. 'What are you asking?'

'Has Simon ever acted aggressively towards you?'

'Not at all. In all the time we've been together, we've never had so much as a cross word.' She shook her head.

'What do you know about him and his family?' Whitney asked.

'I do know that if it hadn't been for his children, he would have left Hannah a long time ago and we would've been together,' she said. 'But he wanted to do the right thing and believed that meant giving them a stable environment with two parents.'

'You didn't agree?' George asked. It annoyed her that she hadn't got the measure of the woman. On the one hand, she was telling the truth about her feelings for Drinkwater, but she seemed to lack remorse for what had happened to his family. If her feelings were strong, she should've shown some empathy for his loss.

'I don't think it's a good idea for children to live in a hostile situation.'

'In what way hostile?' Whitney asked.

'I didn't mean hostile in that they argued but if one person was unhappy, like Simon, then surely the children would have picked up on it.'

'Going back to when you were in London, please run through the whole itinerary,' Whitney said.

'We arrived Sunday afternoon and stayed at the Harvest on Sunday and Monday nights. We were due to stay Tuesday and Wednesday also, but Simon was called back on Tuesday morning because of the fire.'

'Were you with him all of the time?'

'You've already asked me that. We were together apart from when he was in training. Is that all? I want to be with Simon as he's very distressed at the moment.'

'Who paid for the hotel room?' Whitney asked.

'He did as it was on expenses.'

'That should be all for now,' Whitney said.

'Thank you,' Charlotte said, standing up.

They escorted her to the entrance and waited until she'd left.

'It looks like he's in the clear unless they were in it together,' Whitney said. 'What do you think?'

'It's a possibility but if they were in London, and the hotel can vouch for them, it's a long way to travel to set the fire and then return,' George said. 'Then again, they could have paid someone to do it for them. Or she could have. She certainly has a motive as she wanted him to be with her all the time. Judging by his reactions, I doubt he was involved, even if she was.'

'It was interesting that she referred to Drinkwater as being a *perfect partner*, as those were the exact words Hannah's friend Scarlett used when she talked about how he was before they had their first child. He changed after that.'

'It certainly indicates a possible pattern.'

'We'd better tell Drinkwater he can leave as we have no reason to hold him. Then I need to get back to the office. I've still got my interview to prepare for and there's less than twenty-four hours to go.'

'As we've got him here, do you want to ask him about the gnome we found in the garden?'

'We might as well to find out if it belonged to the children, although I can't help feeling that we're clutching at straws.'

They headed back to where Drinkwater had been left and went in together.

'About time,' he grumbled as they walked in.

'We have a further question.' Whitney started the recording equipment. 'Interview resumed. Dr Cavendish in place of Detective Sergeant Price. Mr Drinkwater, we'd like to ask you about the garden gnome in your front garden.'

He rubbed his chin. 'What?'

'There was a garden gnome on the grass.'

'It's not ours. It must have blown in from someone else's garden.'

'That's unlikely as there have been no gales recently.'

'It's still not ours.'

Whitney pulled out her phone and pulled up a photo of the object. 'Look.' She held out her phone.

'I've never seen it before in my life.'

'Could one of the children have put it there and put a scarf on it?'

'I doubt it. We don't have a garden gnome.'

'Do you recognise the scarf wrapped around it?'

'Why are you bothering over a stupid garden gnome, what's it got to do with the fire?' He thumped the table and glared at Whitney.

'Thank you,' she said, in a level voice. 'That will be all for now. You may leave.'

'Good,' he snapped.

He slid back in his chair, making a loud scraping noise, and marched out of the interview room.

'Thoughts?' Whitney said, turning to George.

'I don't think he's involved.'

'I'm inclined to agree with you, which means we're three fires in and still no closer to solving the case.'

TWENTY

Thursday, 24 September

'They're ready for you now.'

Whitney glanced at the chief constable's personal assistant who had called her into the interview and sucked in a breath. She stood up, pulling at her skirt so it hung straight. She'd worn three-inch heels to make her appear taller and more commanding, determined not to let them intimidate her. Not that she knew who *they* were as she hadn't been informed who was on the interview panel.

'Thank you,' she said, as she straightened her back and walked in with purpose.

She hoped to exude an air of confidence, despite the fact she was shitting herself, but she wasn't going to let them see. Behind the table were four people. The HR director, the chief constable, assistant chief constable and, judging from her uniform, a superintendent who she didn't recognise.

'Please take a seat,' the chief constable, Sandra Littleton, said.

The door behind her closed as she sat.

'Thank you for coming in for the interview,' the officer she didn't recognise said. 'I'm Detective Superintendent Helen Clyde, and you know the other members of the panel.'

Whitney nodded at all of them. Was she meant to reply?

'As you know,' Littleton said. 'Lenchester force is amalgamating with Willsden and there's going to be a restructure. I'm going to start with the hardest question. What would your reaction be if you were no longer responsible for a CID team and had a different position within the force?'

Bloody hell, she wasn't wrong that they were starting with the hardest question. Hardly good HR interview practice. Did the HR director approve of this? She glanced at him, but his head was bowed, appearing to look at the open folder in front of him. Her details, no doubt. Was there anything in there about her altercations with Dickhead Douglas? She mentally shook herself. Why would there be? Nothing was ever recorded.

She swallowed hard while formulating her response. 'I would be disappointed, naturally. But it would depend on what the position was, and the opportunities it gave me.'

That was a total lie as all she wanted was to carry on with her team. Thank goodness George wasn't on the panel.

'At present, we're not in a position to make offers to individual officers. Those discussions will take place following all of the interviews,' Littleton said.

'I understand,' Whitney replied. 'Have you decided on the overall structure yet?'

'That much we can tell you,' the chief constable said, smiling. 'I'll hand you over to Detective Superintendent Clyde as she's part of the restructure planning group.'

Whitney scrutinised the officer. Despite sitting she could tell she was tall. Her dark hair was cut into a short sleek bob and tucked behind her ears. Not a hair was out of place. What role was she going to have in the amalgamated force?

'Thank you,' Clyde said. 'We're going to rationalise the

number of detective chief inspectors we have on the merged force. DCIs are currently undertaking work that could be done just as effectively by inspectors. This move will enable us to deal with budgetary restrictions placed on us by government.'

Whitney couldn't spot any accent. Private school? Fast track? It would be just her luck. She hoped their paths didn't cross.

'I see,' Whitney said.

'Would you be interested in a more administrative position?' Clyde asked, her grey eyes locking with Whitney's.

More admin? The thought sent shivers down her spine.

'I would consider anything offered to me, ma'am,' she replied, smiling.

What choice did she have? She certainly wasn't going to tell them she'd rather crawl over hot coals than be stuck behind a desk pushing paper.

'That's good to know,' Clyde said.

'We are interviewing DCIs from both forces, as you know,' Littleton said.

'Yes, ma'am,' she said.

'As Detective Superintendent Clyde has explained, there are too many DCIs to fill the number of positions we have. But that doesn't mean there won't be other opportunities. We are working with West Mercia Police to redeploy officers we're unable to offer positions to. Plus, we're expecting some voluntary redundancies. We will be running a tight ship, and budgetary considerations are paramount.'

'Yes, ma'am,' Whitney said, not wishing to comment, as she absorbed the possibilities. What would be worse: admin or West Mercia? There wasn't a choice. She wasn't prepared to move, but she'd keep that to herself.

The one thing she'd learnt about interviews she'd had in the past was, within reason, the less she said the better, in case she dropped herself in it. Her fists were clenched in her lap, but she uncoiled her fingers, to ensure she appeared relaxed.

'Now we've got that out of the way, I would like to ask you about your position as a detective chief inspector. You've been in that role for a number of years. Why have you not applied for promotion?' Littleton asked.

'I'm happy where I am. I like working on the ground and don't wish to do more paperwork than is necessary.' Crap. Why the hell did she say that?

'Do you struggle with the administrative side of the job?' the HR director asked.

'Not at all,' she replied, looking at him and smiling. 'I do all the administrative work that's required of me.' She'd remembered just in time not to call it paper-pushing. 'But I also like to be out with my team doing what I do best, which is investigating crimes.'

'Thank you for your honesty.' He coughed and glanced down at the open file on the table in front of him. 'I understand you haven't always seen eye to eye with your superior officers.'

She clamped her mouth shut. Who blabbed? Jamieson, no doubt. Why he felt the need to put the knife in, she didn't know. Their clear-up rate was solid, thanks to her team and he should respect that.

'That's not entirely true. There have been some instances when I voiced my opinion, despite it being different from the person I was talking to, but it hasn't been an issue.' Did that make her sound like a pain in the arse to her superiors?

'We understand, in particular, you've had issues with Chief Superintendent Douglas.'

What the ... He was a chief superintendent now? How the hell had that happened? The last she heard, Dickhead Douglas was a Detective Superintendent, the same as Jamieson. Surely, she couldn't be the only one who saw him for who he really was?

'What made you say that?' she asked, in a soft voice, forcing herself not to let her true feelings for him show.

'We were at a police conference together. When we spoke about the amalgamation of the two forces your name came up.'

She certainly wasn't going to tell them the reason behind their *issue*. When he was a sergeant, and she was new in the job, he'd sexually harassed her. She'd told him, in no uncertain terms, where to go. He'd never forgiven her. There had been a couple of instances when their paths had crossed since and both times he'd attempted to derail her career.

'Is Chief Superintendent Douglas going to be part of the amalgamated force?' she asked, hoping her anxiety didn't show.

'Decisions regarding the top positions haven't been made, yet,' Littleton said.

What would she do if he ended up there? She'd have to leave. She could get a job as a private investigator, or the head of security somewhere. Something. Anything.

'Going back to your issues with superiors—'

'I would disagree that I have had any issues,' she said interrupting the HR director. 'Chief Superintendent Douglas and I did have a problem over ten years ago, but that's over and done with and has no bearing on my ability to do the job.'

'I'd like to ask about your team,' the assistant chief constable said. 'You've had a team of officers working with you for several years now.'

'Yes.'

'There's every likelihood that some of them won't be offered a position in the new force. If you had to select those who would continue working in your team, would you be able to make that decision?'

'Are you asking me to choose those who will continue working here?'

They all had their special qualities. Choosing them wouldn't be an easy task.

'No. They will each have their interviews with an interview panel. We wanted to elicit your view on who should stay and who should go.'

'They're an excellent team. Hard-working and loyal. At the nucleus are a few people who all have their own individual skill set. DC Ellie Naylor is an exceptional researcher. I would keep her on the team.'

'What about your sergeant, Matthew Price?'

'He's a very good officer.'

'Why hasn't he taken his inspector's exams?'

'There are personal reasons for that,' she said, instantly wanting to kick herself for opening her mouth. 'But that hasn't affected his ability to do the job.'

The interview continued for a further thirty minutes during which time they discussed her skill sets and posed a variety of different scenarios for her to consider and make recommendations. She breathed a sigh of relief once it was over.

Whatever happened there was nothing she could do about it now. She could have killed Dickhead for mentioning her in a derogatory way but hopefully the panel would be able to see beyond that.

She glanced at her watch, it was already six and she could do with a stiff drink. She pulled out her phone and called George.

'Hello, how did it go?' were George's first words on answering.

'As expected. I'm glad it's over. I'm knackered. These things always take it out of you. Are you free for a drink by any chance?'

'Why don't you come here, and I'll cook us dinner. You can tell me all about it then.'

She couldn't think of a better way to spend an evening.

'Fantastic. I need to unwind, big time.'

TWENTY-ONE

Thursday, 24 September

Thirty minutes after George had spoken to Whitney there was a knock at the door. The officer stood on the doorstep, her face tense.

'Are you okay?' George asked.

'I'm fine. I just need a drink,' Whitney replied, walking into the hall and holding out a bottle of wine. 'I stopped at the off-licence for this as I think it might be a long night.'

'But you're driving,' George said.

'I can always get a taxi if I have too much. I'm hoping this will calm me down.'

'Come on through. I'm just making a sauce to go with the tagliatelle. I know it's one of your favourites.' It was fortunate she had all the ingredients in her pantry.

Whitney gave her a hug and she froze. 'You know I love you. You're such a great friend.'

No one had ever said that to her before.

They went into the kitchen and she took the wine from Whitney and put it into the fridge.

'It's not the right temperature,' she said, as Whitney stared at her, her lips set in a thin line.

'But I got it from the fridge, not the shelf, as I know what you're like.'

'There's some chilled wine in the fridge, we'll start with that.'

'Okay, as long as I'm not expected to wait for a glass.'

George took the quarter-full bottle from the previous evening with Ross and poured them both a glass. Whitney sat at the table and drunk nearly half of it in one go.

'Steady on, it's meant to be savoured.'

'Then you've given it to the wrong person.'

'I think you might have to stay here overnight,' George said.

She kept the bed made up in the spare bedroom, so it wouldn't be an issue for her friend to stay.

'I can get a taxi. Plus, I've only drunk half a glass. I needed the initial hit, to calm me.'

George stood at the hob, stirring the sauce. 'Tell me what happened.'

'It was the interview from hell.'

'I'm sure it wasn't that bad. We're very often not the best judge of how well we perform in certain situations, interviews being one of them.'

'Normally, I'd agree with you, but this was different. I'd prepared for it and thought it was going okay until they mentioned Dickhead Douglas.' Whitney screwed up her face. 'You're not going to believe this. He's now been promoted to *Chief Superintendent* and it's possible he'll be working at the new station.'

'They told you that, did they?' she asked.

'No, but it would be just my luck for that to happen.' Whitney thumped the table.

'You're jumping the gun here. Did they give any indication

that he would return to Lenchester or is it you making an unin-
formed leap?' George asked, trying to help.

'No, they didn't say it was going to happen, or even suggest
it might, but can you imagine if he came back into my life? I'd
have to leave the force as I couldn't be within spitting distance
of the arsewipe.'

'Don't make any rash decisions. Wait until you know for
sure. What questions did they ask?'

She reached over for the kettle, filled it with water, and set it
to boil.

'Difficult ones. They even asked me about the team and
who I'd select to keep.'

What was the problem with that?

'That is an obvious question to ask of someone in your position,' she pointed out, unsure whether she was helping or not. It
seemed that Whitney wasn't prepared to listen to logic and
instead wanted to vent her feelings on the whole proceedings.

'Maybe it was, but I wasn't going to give them any ammunition to work with. I simply explained what a good team they are.
They don't want me to interview them for their posts.'

'It's over now. You have to put it out of your mind, as there's
nothing further you can do.'

'You and your compartmentalising. I keep telling you, it's
not easy for me to do. I can't stop the thoughts coming into my
head.'

'You have to train yourself. It can be done. Trust me on this,'
she said, wondering what her friend would say if she realised
that George had been unable to follow her own advice when it
came to Ross.

'I'll take your word for it, but at the moment, all I want to do
is sit here and drown my sorrows. I'm glad you were here so I
could come and talk to you.'

'It's my pleasure. Dinner's almost ready.'

George served up and while eating they discussed Tiffany.

Whitney was concerned about when she should tell her daughter about her father considering she had no idea who he was, or that he was back on the scene.

She was pleased to see that Whitney was still on her first glass of wine by the end of the meal and didn't get drunk. George loaded the dishwasher and they took their coffee into the sitting room.

'So, tell me about you and Ross,' Whitney said.

'I was wondering when you were going to get on to that,' George said arching an eyebrow.

'Am I that predictable?' Whitney said, smiling, as she took a sip of coffee.

'Yes, you are. I've decided to see him again, but to take it steady. I have missed him, but I'm not jumping back in to how it was before.'

'Honestly, sometimes I could give you a good shake. You've missed him. He's clearly *the one*, yet you're talking about holding him at arm's length.'

'No, I'm not. I'm not you. I'm not emotional. I take my time, to work situations out.'

'If you say so. I—' Whitney paused. 'It's ten o'clock. Where did the time go?'

'We were talking,' George said.

'Trust you to state the obvious.' Whitney grinned. Her phone rang and she picked it up and looked at the screen. 'It's work. Walker,' she said answering it. 'What? Not again. We'll be there straight away.' Whitney finished the call as the colour drained from her face.

'What is it?' she asked.

'Another fire. It's at a night club on Wellington Road where there was a party taking place. I can't believe it. Come on.'

'We'll go in my car,' she said.

'I've only had one glass, I'm not over the limit.'

'I know. I thought you'd want to go in mine as usual.'

* * *

The journey to the party, which was in an underground club, took twenty-five minutes. When they arrived, there were small clusters of people staring at the building. The club entrance was situated between two shops, both of which were burnt out. The flames had been extinguished but there was smoke still billowing. There were three fire engines and two ambulances, and the area was cordoned off.

They went over and ducked under the tape. Whitney held out her warrant card as they reached one of the fire officers.

'Tell me what's happening,' Whitney said.

'The fire was started at the rear of the building, and very quickly spread to the front entrance.'

'Shit. How many bodies?'

'We're still bringing them out. There are quite a few alive who have been taken to hospital. I'm hoping there will be more.'

'Isn't there another exit, in case of fire?'

'There is, but it looks like it wasn't used. Beer crates were blocking it. How the hell they passed a fire inspection beats me.' He let out an exasperated sigh.

'We'll leave you to it,' she said as she turned to George. 'Let's have a look round.' She took out her phone and recorded the groups of people milling around.

'Do you want to speak to some of the onlookers?' George asked.

'Yes. Let's go over there,' Whitney said pointing to where there were three young girls sobbing.

'I'm Detective Chief Inspector Walker,' Whitney said, when they reached them. 'Do you know anyone who was at the party?'

'Yes,' one of the girls said, sniffing. 'We would have been there, too, if we hadn't been late.'

'What can you tell me about the party?'

'It was a twenty-first for our friend Janelle Jackson, she ...' her voice broke.

'Do you know who was invited?' Whitney asked, gently.

'Friends and family.'

'How do you know Janelle?'

'We're all studying at Lenchester uni, together.' A loud sob erupted from her, and another of the girls put her arm around her shoulder.

'If you can give me your details and then I suggest you all go home. There's no point in hanging around here because it's going to take a while for the fire brigade to get the situation under control and also get everyone out,' Whitney said gently. She pulled out her notebook and took the details of the three girls, and then they left.

She turned to George. 'This makes me so sick. If this too is arson, then it could be someone who knew about the party?'

'It seems likely,' George said.

'Come on, let's go. You'll be a wreck tomorrow if you don't go home and get some sleep.'

'I'll be fine. I'm not at work tomorrow.'

'Why not?'

'I've been instructed to use up some of my annual leave entitlement as we're not allowed to carry it over. I've taken the day off.'

'You'll be able to have a lie-in. Some of us won't be so lucky.'

TWENTY-TWO

Friday, 25 September

Whitney stifled a yawn as she walked into the incident room. She'd been up late after the fire, unable to sleep, and now had come in early to speak to the team to move the investigation forward.

She headed first into her office. There was an email from Roger, the FIO, asking her to call as soon as possible.

'It's DCI Whitney Walker,' she said after he'd answered.

'Good morning. Rather than waiting for the official report, I wanted to let you know that the investigation into the fire in Rushmere Close has identified the cause as being the same as the first two. Very early findings on last night's fire indicate same again.'

'We've definitely got a serial arsonist,' she said.

'Yeah.'

'How many fatalities were there from last night?'

'Ten dead, most of them from the same family. Fifty survived and all were taken to the hospital. Eight of them are still there and the others have been discharged. It could have been so much worse if we hadn't got there so promptly. I'll forward you a list of names.'

'Thanks, Roger. I appreciate you letting me know.'

'You're welcome.'

She ended the call and walked into the incident room, where most of the team were already working. 'Good morning, everyone. I've been speaking with the fire investigator and he informed me that ten people died in last night's fire.'

'For fuck's sake,' Doug said. 'This can't go on. That makes it twenty-seven people who have died at the hands on this bastard.'

'We're doing the best we can,' Frank said.

'It's not good enough,' Doug replied.

'I understand,' Whitney said, gently. 'We'll catch this person, but we can't let our emotions get in the way as it will cloud our judgement. It's also been confirmed that the first three fires, and most likely the one from last night, were carried out by the same person, or persons. Has any new information come in since yesterday afternoon?'

'I've heard back from the ambulance service, regarding the paramedic who was at the second and third fire, guv,' Frank said. 'He wasn't on duty for the first one. I've also checked with the fire service, and there was no one who attended all of the fires.'

'Thanks, Frank. It was certainly worth considering. Anyone else?'

'Yes, guv,' Ellie said. 'Barry, from forensics, has been in touch regarding the gnome you found in the Drinkwaters' garden. It wasn't a scarf wrapped around it, but a gang bandana which they've linked to the *Lenchester Reds*.'

'Bloody hell,' Frank said. 'Don't tell me they're involved in the fires. Their leader is Darren Hunt, also known as Daz. He has a record as long as your arm. From grievous bodily harm to petty arson as a teenager. I remember before he started the gang. A right little so-and-so. They're not big players though, so what's the connection?'

Whitney let out a long sigh, thankful that they now had something to work on.

'That's what we need to find out. I want him brought in here pronto. Matt, get uniform to collect him.'

'Yes, guv.'

'Doug and Sue, I want you to follow up on last night's fire. It was a private party for a student named Janelle Jackson. The fire officer is sending me a list of fatalities and survivors. Frank, the fire started at the rear of the building, check the CCTV footage there. Ellie, find out what you can about Darren Hunt.'

'Yes, guv.'

She returned to her office and pulled out her phone to call George.

'Sorry, it's early. How busy are you?' she said when the psychologist answered.

'I was about to do some gardening and then had planned to give Ross a call.'

'I wondered if you could come in as we've had a break. It wasn't a scarf wrapped around the gnome, but a bandana belonging to a local gang. The leader, Darren Hunt, is being brought in for questioning. We've also had confirmation that all of the fires have the same MO.'

'Give me forty-five minutes and I'll be with you. I need to change as I'm in my gardening gear.'

Whitney smiled to herself. She was sure the *gardening gear* would be fine. George was always immaculately turned out. She'd never seen the woman scruffy in the whole time she'd known her.

'Okay. I'll see you soon.'

'Guv,' Ellie called out. 'I've got something.'

Whitney hurried over to the officer. 'Tell me.'

'Darren Hunt was brought up in foster care in Bristol, with

his sister, Suzanne, who's two years younger. When they were teenagers, they set fire to one of the homes they were fostered into.'

'Excellent,' Whitney said, doing a fist pump. 'Find out what you can about the sister.'

'I have already,' Ellie said, smirking, clearly pleased with herself. 'She no longer goes by the name Suzanne Hunt. Now she's known as Charlotte Payne.'

What the ...

'Simon Drinkwater's mistress? Good work, Ellie.' She beamed at the officer.

'We've got something,' she called out to the rest of the team. 'It's possible that all of the fires have been a distraction to put us off knowing who the intended victims really were. Hannah Drinkwater, and her two children. The other deaths were designed to muddy the waters. Matt, I want you and Frank to take some uniformed officers and go to Charlotte Payne's house in Rugby. Bring in Drinkwater, too. He might be involved. Make sure they're in separate cars. I don't want them to have time to jointly concoct a story. At last we're getting somewhere. I'll let Jamieson know.'

'Yes, guv,' Matt said.

Whitney marched out of the incident room and hurried upstairs. Jamieson was sitting in his office staring into space. How many times had she seen him doing that recently? It was definitely odd.

She tapped gently on the open door and walked in. 'Sir, we have a development in the case.'

'Come in Walker.'

'The fire service has confirmed that all of the fires were set in the same manner, however, we believe they were a screen to hide the intended victims. Hannah Drinkwater and her children. A bandana linked to the *Lenchester Reds* was left at the scene. The leader of the gang is the brother of Simon Drinkwater's mistress. We don't know if he was in on it, but we're bringing in Darren Hunt, the gang leader, and also Drinkwater, and his mistress.'

'Okay. Keep me informed.'

Is that all he had to say? Usually he was more vocal.

'Is everything all right, sir?' she asked.

She couldn't help herself however much they didn't get on.

'Nothing you can help me with, Walker.'

'Is it to do with the merger?' she asked, having a guess.

'Well, obviously that's what it is, because that's what's on everybody's mind,' he barked. 'I've got a decision to make.'

And now he was back to normal.

'I'm here if you need to talk,' she said immediately regretting it. Why on earth had she said that?

'It's not appropriate for me to discuss these things with someone in your position. How did your interview go?'

'Didn't they tell you?' That was a surprise.

'No, why would they?'

'As my superior officer, I'd have thought you'd have been informed. Did they ask you for a reference?'

'They have spoken to me regarding you, and your record.'

Her insides clenched. What had he said?

'Do you know when we'll find out about the new teams?'

'I've no idea but, again, I'm not going to discuss it with you. You'll have to wait, like the rest of us.'

TWENTY-THREE

Friday, 25 September

George parked in the station car park and hurried into the incident room. Whitney was nowhere to be seen, so she carried on to her office and found her there sitting at her desk.

'Is everything okay?' she asked.

'Yes, it's fine. I was thinking about the future of my team. I'm glad you're here to take my mind off it.'

'Is Hunt here yet?' she asked.

'Yes, he's just arrived,' Whitney said. 'We've had a further development. He has a sister, only she doesn't go by the name Hunt, she's changed it to ... wait for it ... Payne. Charlotte Payne.'

'Simon Drinkwater's girlfriend? Now it's beginning to make sense.'

'We've brought her, and Drinkwater, in for questioning, too.'

'Are you working on the assumption they're in it together?' George asked, curious to find out whether she and Whitney were on the same page.

'It certainly looks that way. Do you have an opinion?' She tilted her head to one side. 'Stupid question,' she added.

'I'm not convinced. If it was only his wife at home, then it would be plausible. But his children? He was devastated when they'd died. His grief wasn't an act, I'm convinced of it.'

'Unless he believed the children wouldn't be there, that they were staying with friends or relatives,' Whitney said.

'Except he'd been in contact with his wife and knew they'd gone out for dinner that evening.'

'According to him. We didn't actually verify that part of his story. He could be covering his bases.'

'Maybe.' George shrugged, still not convinced.

'We'll find out when we interview Drinkwater and Payne. But first we're going to question Darren Hunt. I'll take Matt and you can observe.'

Darren Hunt was thickset, with a suntan and shaved head. He sat at the table with his muscly tattooed arms folded across his chest. When Whitney and Matt walked in, George observed his top lip curl.

'Why am I here?' he demanded before they'd even sat down.

'We have questions for you,' Whitney said, flatly, as she turned on the recording equipment. 'Friday twenty-fifth of September, those present: Detective Chief Inspector Walker, Detective Sergeant Price. State your name,' she said to Hunt.

'Daz Hunt.'

'Full name.'

'Darren Johnathon Hunt,' he said, emphasising each syllable.

'Mr Hunt, I understand you're the leader of the *Lenchester Reds*. Is that true?'

'Yes.'

'Is this your gang's bandana?' She took a photo from the file in front of her and slid it over.

'Yes.'

'How did it come to be in the garden of 9 Rushmere Close, Lenchester?'

'I don't know.'

'Do you know who lived at the address?'

'No.'

'Simon Drinkwater and his family.'

'He knows the name,' George said. 'His eyes flickered when you mentioned it.'

'Hannah Drinkwater and her two children recently died in a fire there.'

'And?'

'*And* a bandana from your gang was found in the garden.'

'That doesn't mean I had anything to do with the fire.'

'Your sister, Suzanne. Or Charlotte, as she's now known, was having an affair with Simon Drinkwater.'

'A coincidence?' Hunt said.

'There's no such thing,' Whitney said.

George smiled. 'Finally, you're coming around to my way of thinking.'

'We are investigating a series of fires which took place on the thirteenth, seventeenth, and twenty-second of September ... and last night. What were you doing on all these dates?'

'Florida. I got back yesterday.'

That accounted for the suntan.

'We will be checking.'

'Be my guest. Now can I go?'

'No. We haven't finished. You could have orchestrated the fires from overseas.'

He slammed his hands on the table, and leant forward, his eyes on Whitney. 'Prove it.'

'We believe that your sister asked you to arrange a series of fires, which resulted in many deaths, to cover the intended victims who were Hannah Drinkwater and her two children. This would then leave it clear for her to move in with Simon Drinkwater.'

Hunt sat back, giving a slow handclap. 'Very inventive. But stupid. As I said before: prove it.'

'Mr Hunt. How did your gang's bandana end up in the Drinkwaters' garden?'

'I've already told you. I don't know.'

'What's the significance of it being tied around a garden gnome?'

'None.'

'So why was it put there?' Whitney asked.

'Enough.' He glared at them. 'I have nothing else to say, so you either let me go or I call my solicitor.'

'Interview suspended,' Whitney said, as she paused the recording. 'Stay here. We'll be back.'

George met them in the corridor. 'I don't believe he was involved as nothing about his behaviour indicated he wasn't telling the truth.'

'We'll leave him there for a while and talk to his sister,' Whitney said.

They headed down the corridor to the interview room where the woman was waiting. George stepped into the observation area and scrutinised Payne for any telltale signs of anxiety. But there were none. The woman sat upright in her chair, looking confident.

Whitney placed her files on the table.

'Why am I here?' Payne demanded, staring directly at Whitney.

'Notice how she's going on the offensive immediately, without giving you a chance to speak. Just like her brother.

Typical behaviour of someone who thinks they're in control,' George said into the mic.

'We wish to speak to you regarding the fire at Simon Drinkwater's home.'

'I've already told you I—'

Whitney held up her hand to silence the woman and then started the recording equipment.

'Interesting,' George said. 'She's gone from offensive to defensive in a matter of seconds.'

The woman wouldn't be easy to crack.

'You mentioned when we interviewed you previously, that you come from Bristol,' Whitney said.

'Yes. So what?'

'Does your family still live there?'

'I have no idea and I fail to see what this has to do with the fire at Simon's house.'

'Is it right that you were brought up in foster care?'

The woman's eyes darted from Whitney to Matt and back again. 'Where did you get that idea from?'

'According to our records you were in foster care for most of your childhood along with your brother, Darren. You also changed your name from Suzanne Hunt to Charlotte Payne.'

'How did you find that out?' She bit down on her bottom lip.

'Now you have her worried,' George said.

'We're the police, of course we're going to find that out. We also understand that you have a police record from when you were a teenager for helping Darren set fire to one of the homes you were fostered in.' Payne sat back and glared at them. 'Please answer the question.'

'There was no question.'

'Ms Payne, can you confirm that you were formerly known as Suzanne Hunt, and that you have a police record for arson?'

'Yes, that's true. Darren set the fire because the bastard man of the house wouldn't leave me alone. It was the only way to stop him.'

'What was he doing?' Whitney asked.

'What do you think?' She glared at Whitney.

'Why did you change your name?'

'To get away from what happened in the past.'

'Yet you live close to your brother and keep in contact with him.'

'So what? It's not a crime.'

'I want to ask you about the fire which killed Hannah Drinkwater and her two children. Did you ask your brother to arrange it and also carry out three other fires as a cover?'

'Of course I didn't. What sort of person do you think I am?'

'Someone who wanted to be with her lover, at all costs?' Whitney said.

'That's crazy.'

'Was Simon involved in it too? Was it something you'd planned to do in order for the two of you to be together?'

'No comment,' Payne said.

'Keep pushing,' George said.

'I'm asking you again. Whose idea was it? Were you in it together? Did Simon force you to arrange with your brother to do it? We know he's got a history of being physically abusive towards his wife.'

'No. No. No. We had nothing to do with the fire, we were in London.' Her face crumpled, and she bowed her head, all fight appearing to have left her body.

'I don't think you're going to get anything else from her now,' George said.

'Interview suspended,' Whitney said halting the recording. 'Wait here.'

George left the observation room and met Whitney and Matt in the corridor.

'All her abrasiveness has subsided. I suspect she's telling the truth.'

'Suspect or know?' Whitney asked, her body tense.

'Obviously, I don't know for sure.'

'Let's talk to Drinkwater and see what he has to say.'

They headed for an interview room further down the corridor and George slipped into the observation area.

Simon Drinkwater was slumped forward. Stubble dotted his chin and his eyes were red-rimmed.

'Take it easy with him,' George said as Whitney and Matt entered the room. 'It appears the enormity of what has happened has hit him. I know you don't have much sympathy for him, but my advice is to show compassion as it will help.'

Whitney placed her folders on the table and gave a sharp nod of her head, her body remaining rigid. It was likely that she'd do as George had suggested, despite her demeanour showing disdain for the man.

After starting the recording, Whitney took out a photo from her folder, leant over, and placed it in front of him. 'Mr Drinkwater, I'd like you to take another look at this garden gnome which was left on your front lawn. Have you seen it before?'

He leant forward and stared. 'Why are you asking me again? I've already said I don't recognise it,' he hesitated. 'Unless it was one of the children's toys.'

'This isn't a toy. It's a garden ornament and tied around it is a gang bandana.'

He looked again. 'In that case, no. It doesn't belong to us.'

'He's still talking as if his family are still alive. He's extremely fragile,' George said.

'I'd like to talk to you about Suzanne Hunt,' Whitney said.

He frowned. 'I don't know her.'

'She now goes by the name Charlotte Payne.'

George gave an exasperated sigh. 'Whitney, I said take it easy on him.'

'I didn't know that,' he said, his tone uncertain.

'The bandana on the garden gnome in the photo is used by members of the *Lenchester Reds.*'

'Who are they?' he asked.

'A local gang.'

'But ...' His voice trailed off.

'The leader of the gang is called Darren Hunt and his sister is the woman you know as Charlotte Payne.'

Drinkwater slumped forward and rested his head in his hands. After a few seconds he sat upright and stared at Whitney and Matt. 'Are you saying that she had something to do with the deaths of Hannah and the children?'

'There is a connection which we're investigating.'

'I can't stay there,' he muttered. 'I have to leave.'

'Mr Drinkwater?'

He glanced at Whitney as if suddenly remembering where he was. 'I'll be moving out of the house in Rugby and booking into a hotel in Lenchester.'

'Make sure to inform us of your new location, once you have it,' Whitney said.

'May I go now?'

'Yes. We have finished questioning you for the moment.' Whitney stopped the recording.

'How am I to get back to Rugby?' he asked.

'I'll arrange for an officer to take you.'

'I don't want to go in the same car as Charlotte,' he said.

'He has a history of physical abuse, you should keep them separate,' George said.

'My officer will take you to Rugby, and wait for you to collect your belongings, before bringing you back to Lenchester. Wait here.'

After Whitney and Matt left the interview room George joined them.

'What is it?' she asked, as Whitney scowled at her.

'Matt, arrange for someone to take Drinkwater.'

'Yes, guv.'

After he had left them, Whitney turned to George. 'Why did you say that?'

'You'll need to explain, as I don't know what you mean?'

'Why did you mention about keeping them separate because of what he's like? Do you think I don't realise? I'm not a total novice.'

'I didn't intend to question your ability. I was just passing comment. I'm sorry if—'

'Stop,' Whitney said, holding up her hand. 'Ignore me. You were doing your job. I'm sorry for snapping. It's this whole bloody situation. The fires. The restructure. The uncertainty. It's doing my head in.'

'You can't hold Hunt, Payne, or Drinkwater as they have alibis and I'm convinced they weren't involved.'

'It's like we're back to square one.'

'Not quite. We still have a link to the gang. We just haven't yet worked out what it is.'

TWENTY-FOUR

'Hold the phone still, or I'll look like I'm shaking, and people will think I'm scared,' I say.

All he has to do is video me telling my story, so it can be added to the footage of the fires being started. Then I'll upload it for the elders in the gang to see. It's not exactly hard but the little shit is going all stupid on me like he's about to cry. I'd do it myself, but I don't have a tripod.

'Right. Press start.'

I wait while he fumbles with the phone.

I clear my throat, ready to start. 'Keep watching and you'll see me setting four fires. Not just any fires. These were big and they hurt. Initiation only needs one, but I want to show you that there's nothing I won't do. Remember who I am. You won't get a better runner than me. I'll help make this gang the best.' I stop talking and walk over to him. 'Play it back,' I demand.

He presses play and I listen. It's good. 'Impressed?' I ask.

He glances down at his phone and shrugs.

'For fuck's sake, don't be such a twat. It's a good job you don't want to join, because they'll never take you.'

I watch the replay one more time.

I'm going down in history. I'll be famous.

I've always wanted to be famous so people stop and stare at me.

I'll be the person who killed more people than anyone else ... ever.

TWENTY-FIVE

Saturday, 26 September

Whitney was seated at her desk by seven-thirty. She hadn't been able to sleep and had decided to come into work early. Despite it being the weekend, she'd told the team they were all expected in work by eight. She'd cancelled all days off until the case was solved. If there were more fires, it wouldn't be because they'd been slack in their investigation.

Her phone rang and she glanced at the screen. It was Martin. Why was he calling so early in the morning?

'Hello,' she said, answering it straightaway.

'I hope I haven't woken you.'

'I've been up hours. I'm at work, sitting at my desk.'

'Oh ... That answers my question then,' he said despondently.

'Which was?'

'I wondered if you were free today and fancied going on a boat trip.'

Typical. The one time she can't possibly get away she gets the chance to go out on the water.

'I'm still working on the arson cases. There have been more fires since we last spoke, and I can't go anywhere until we've solved them.'

'I totally understand. You must be under immense pressure.'

It was kind of him to be concerned. 'It's the story of my life. Lenchester's known as *serial killer central*. Daily pressure is a part of it. You didn't tell me you had a boat.'

'I wish. It's not mine, I received a last-minute invite from a client, asking if I'd like to join him on his new luxury yacht. He said I could bring someone with me, and I thought of you.'

Warmth flooded through her. Could he be any better?

'Under normal circumstances, I'd have loved to. But ...' Her words hung in the air.

'Another time then,' he said, sighing. 'How did your interview go?'

She smiled to herself. He'd remembered. 'Honestly, I have no idea. I've been over it in my head so many times, it's impossible to make a judgement. Sometimes it feels like I nailed it, and others that I totally screwed it up. The truth is, though, nailing it might mean I end up doing more paper-pushing.'

'I can't envision you being happy with that.'

She gave a hollow laugh. 'You've got it in one. I want to be out there solving cases and working with my team.'

'Did you tell the interview panel that?'

'What do you think? Of course not. I made out I'd be happy with any position. I can't leave Lenchester which basically means taking whatever I'm offered. *If* I'm offered, that is.'

'I'm sure you will be. It would be ridiculous to let someone of your ability go.'

'We'll see. Sorry, I've got to go as my team is due in soon. Enjoy going out on the yacht. I'm extremely envious.'

'Hopefully he'll extend another invite, at a time when you

can come with me. Don't forget to call when you hear about your job.'

'I won't.'

'And don't forget you're coming here for a visit once the case is over,' he added.

Her heart flipped at the thought of it. 'I'm looking forward to it.'

She ended the call and stared at the phone. She couldn't believe how well it was going with him. Once it was all out in the open with Tiffany, and then her mum and brother, she'd be happy. She didn't like keeping secrets.

At a few minutes after eight she went into the incident room and was pleased to see that everyone was seated at their desks.

'Morning,' she said. 'Sorry if you've had to cancel plans, but we're on this case twenty-four-seven until it's solved.'

'I take it you'll be telling the wife, guv, as she's not happy,' Frank said.

'I'd have thought she'd have been glad to see the back of you,' Doug said.

'Very funny,' the older detective replied. 'We were meant to be going to Northampton to visit her sister who's been in hospital.'

'Can't she drive herself?' Doug asked.

'She can, but she has zero sense of direction and is scared she'll get lost.'

'That's what satnav is for.'

'She doesn't have it in her Mini.' He sighed. 'And before you say it, her phone dates back to the ark and doesn't have it on there either.'

'You can send my apologies,' Whitney said, interrupting them as they'd be at it all day if she didn't. 'In the meantime, we're going to go over each fire in turn to refresh our memories of where we are on everything.'

'I don't think we'll forget anything, guv. We've never had so many bodies before,' Frank said.

She walked over to the board and stood beside it, choosing not to answer Frank as it would waste more time and she wanted to get started. 'Fire one in Stanton Road, where Cara and Hamish died' – she pointed to the photo of the burnt-out house – 'initially we suspected the landlord, Sidney Drake who was in financial difficulties and might have set the fire to claim the insurance, but we found no link between him and the other fires.' She crossed his name off the board. 'Matt, you were speaking to the other two students who were to share the house with our victims this academic year, what did they say?'

'They were devastated by what had happened and couldn't think of anyone who might have it in for Cara and Hamish.'

'Thanks. It was a long shot, anyway. Doug, did the Dorset police revisit Hamish's parents?'

'Yes, guv, and they had no idea why their son and his girl-friend were targeted.'

'Okay. Fire two at the factory where we had twelve people die and two survive. Aimee Edwards and Gavin Curtis, who were having an affair. We initially suspected Dale Edwards, Aimee's husband, who was a gambler and had been following the pair, as he suspected them of being in a relationship. He could have started the first fire to put us off the scent. Except he had an ironclad alibi. So, bearing in mind that we know from the fire service that all of the fires were caused by the same person, or persons, then we should rule him out of the equation.' She put a line through his name. 'Fire three—'

'This is key,' Matt interrupted. 'Because of the gang component.'

'I agree,' Frank said.

'It's not a foregone conclusion. We still need to discuss each fire and get everything clear. So, fire three resulted in the deaths of Hannah Drinkwater and her two children, Lucy and Oscar.'

'Targeting kids like that makes me sick,' Doug snarled.

'We'll get the bastard,' Frank said.

'Back to the fire,' Whitney said, wanting to keep them focused. 'The husband, his mistress and her brother, who is the leader of the *Lenchester Reds*, have been eliminated from our enquiries, but we still have the gang bandana left on a garden gnome to consider. And now for the nightclub fire, which was set during a twenty-first party for Janelle Jackson. Ten people died and fifty survived. Where are we in the investigation?'

'Of the eight people who were in hospital, only two are still in there, both in a stable condition,' Sue said.

'Thank goodness,' she said. 'Who checked out the owner of the premises?'

'I did, guv,' Doug said. 'He lives in Spain and is financially secure, so there would be no reason for the fire to be set for insurance purposes. I also spoke to Janelle Jackson, who escaped unharmed. She's devastated, obviously, and can't think of any reason for her being targeted.'

'Thanks, Doug. Frank what did you get from the CCTV?'

'There were no cameras around the back of the building, so it wasn't possible to see anyone there who might have been responsible for setting the fire.'

'Damn.' She grimaced. 'What about the student angle as two of the fires have involved them? I want someone looking into the possibility of a link with the university, however tenuous it might be.'

'I'll do that guv,' Sue said.

'Thanks. Now we're up to date we can move forward with clear heads. I want one hundred per cent focus. We're going to crack this case. We haven't been beaten before, and we won't be now.'

TWENTY-SIX

Saturday, 26 September

When George had received the urgent call from Whitney, she'd dropped everything to come and help. The officer was operating an *all hands on deck* approach until the case was solved, and that included George, whenever possible.

'George, over here,' Whitney shouted from where she was standing next to Matt.

'How can I help?' George asked when she reached them, while trying not to think of all the things she'd planned to do today. Her garden was a mass of weeds, and her house in need of cleaning.

'I'm not going to let this case beat us. I wanted to discuss the arsonist. Do you think he's working to some sort of plan?'

She shook her head. 'There's been no pattern between the fires in terms of the length of time between them, or the locations. Without wanting to stereotype, it's behaviour I'd attribute more to a younger person.'

'Could you talk to the team about the type of person we're

looking for? Do you have anything to add following the last time you spoke to them?'

'I'd be happy to. I've been doing further research into the psychology of arsonists, I'll discuss that,' she said.

Whitney turned to face the team. 'Dr Cavendish has more to add about arsonists.'

George headed over towards the board so she could face the team. 'Good morning. Following on from what I have previously explained to you, I'd like to add more detail.' She tried not to make her voice sound like she was giving a lecture but was unsure whether she'd succeeded. No doubt Whitney would tell her. 'My research into the psychological profiling of arsonists has indicated that most of them have a below average IQ. But I caveat that, as the majority of arsonists aren't caught.'

'Does that mean the low IQ was the reason they were caught, so we can't automatically assume our arsonist falls into that category,' Whitney said.

'Exactly. But it's still useful to know. A further consideration is the notion of anger. Again, research has indicated a primary motivator for an arsonist is anger.'

'Anger directed at who?' Matt asked. 'It can't be the people who died, as they all came from different areas of the city and had no connection with one another.'

'They could be angry with life and their situation. Remember, most arsonists are young men. There are many reasons for the anger they're experiencing. They may have been neglected as young children or have a history of abuse and humiliation. These are factors to bear in mind when conducting the investigation.'

She glanced at Whitney, who was nodding in agreement.

'Thank you, George. You've added another dimension.'

Whitney headed over to her.

'I've also been considering why the bandana was left on the gnome and I've made an assertion—'

'Hold that thought,' Whitney said interrupting her. 'Before you go back to work, Dr Cavendish is going to talk to us about garden gnomes.'

'Is that another of your specialist subjects?' Frank said, smirking.

'Enough, Frank,' Whitney said, rolling her eyes. 'Please continue, George.'

'Garden gnomes aren't simply figurines. There's a history attached to them going back to the ancient Romans.'

'You've got to be kidding me?' Frank said. 'I just thought they were ugly looking ornaments people put in their gardens.'

'Some people may view them as such, but historically, they were considered to be lucky charms, protecting their owners from evil spirits. In respect of the fire, it's possible that the bandana was placed around it to make a point, albeit a misplaced one. It could be that the owner of the bandana is stating nothing can protect a person from the gang.'

'Why misplaced?' Whitney asked.

'Because the family didn't own the gnome. Traditionally, it's only lucky for the person who owns it.'

'But we've already ascertained that Darren Hunt wasn't involved.'

'He wasn't, but that doesn't mean another gang member wasn't,' George said.

'You've previously said that most fires are committed by young males, but surely kids of that age wouldn't be aware of gnome history and how adding the bandana is making a statement. It's too academic.'

Whitney made a solid point.

'That's correct, but I didn't want to discount it. When we have the culprit in custody it's an avenue you'll be able to pursue.'

'Thank you. Is that it, or do you have anything else to tell us?'

'One of my PhD students is researching gang culture, if you're interested in knowing more about his findings.'

'Fire away, the more we know the better if it's going to help solve this case. Although, remember the *Lenchester Reds* are a very small fish in the gang pond.'

'I'll keep it brief, because I know you all want to get on. But it might help in the investigation if you know a little more about how gangs operate. There are different roles and levels of authority within gangs, which are based on the age of the member. They recruit children who can be under ten years old.'

'Seriously?' Ellie asked.

'Yes,' Frank said. 'They use them to carry drugs and weapons, knowing that they're unlikely to be stopped.'

'You know all of this?' George asked.

'When you've been in the force as long as I have, there isn't much you haven't come across. They use kids between twelve and fifteen to actually sell the drugs on the street. There's no hope for many of them once they're entrenched in the gang.'

'Frank's right. Once these children are a part of gang culture, it's where they will probably remain. I probably can't add much that you don't already know, and I'm sure the DCI wants you all to get back to work, so I'll end the lecture ... sorry, not lecture, I was forgetting where I was.' She looked across at Whitney who was grinning.

'Are you going to be setting us homework, now?' her friend asked.

'My dog ate mine,' Frank quipped.

Everyone laughed, and George joined in. She'd miss the camaraderie if the team was disbanded in the restructure.

'Okay. Fun time over. I want everyone to go back over the evidence we do have. The CCTV footage. The interviews. Responses from the public. We have four fires and that should provide us with plenty to work on. There's something we're missing, and we need to find it.' Whitney turned to George.

'Let's go to my office and take another look at the videos I made with my phone.'

George followed Whitney into her office and sat next to her while they looked closely at the recordings of people at the factory fire.

George squinted. 'What's that over there?' She pointed to a couple of shadows on the footage.

'I'm not sure,' Whitney said as she leant in closer.

'It looks like a couple of young boys standing together against a wall.'

'I think you're right. Why didn't we see them before?'

'They're hard to spot. I only noticed it because I'm not looking at the screen head on like you are. I'm at a slight angle because of where I'm sitting.'

'Let's take a look at the recording from the Drinkwaters' house and see if we can spot the same shadows.' Whitney brought up the recording, but they didn't see anything. 'Damn.'

'They could be hiding behind cars, or around the corner,' George said. 'Let's look at the footage from the nightclub.'

'Okay,' Whitney said, calling it up.

They stared in silence, and George slowly examined the screen. 'That could be them,' she said, pointing at a couple of people. 'It's hard to tell as we're looking at shadows. How are we going to find out?'

'I'll get Ellie onto it. I'm not sure whether we're going to be able to identify them because we can't actually see the faces.'

'What about CCTV footage close to the party?'

'Frank would have examined that. We'll go and see what he found.'

They returned to the incident room and Whitney went over to Ellie.

'Take a look at the recordings I made at the factory and the nightclub. We've spotted a couple of shadows which we think could be two boys. See if it's possible to identify them.'

'Yes, guv.'

'Frank,' Whitney called out as they headed over to his desk. 'When you checked the CCTV footage, did you see any young people close to the factory and the nightclub?'

'Two teenage boys were walking in the direction of the nightclub half an hour before the fire started but they didn't stay for long. I'll call up the relevant footage up for you to see.' They waited while he found the right frames. 'There they are.' He pointed at the screen. 'See, they walked past and kept on going. They didn't even stop to stare at the doorway, so I didn't think it relevant.'

'It might not be, but if it was them and they were being careful, they could have doubled back once the fire ignited so they could survey their handiwork. If they were to go around the back of the building could they do so without being caught on camera?'

'Yes and no,' Frank said.

'What's that meant to mean?'

'There isn't a road which leads directly to the rear of the building containing the nightclub but, if they know the area, there's an alleyway along Weston Street that runs parallel to Wellington Road. At the end of the alley is a six-foot wall separating it from the car park used by the shops and club. If they managed to scale it, then they could've got in without being spotted.'

'Guv,' Ellie called out, diverting their attention. 'It's impossible to identify them because we can't see their faces from any angle.'

'Okay, it was worth trying.' She gave a frustrated sigh. 'Let's look at the two boys walking past the club again. They look about the same height as those on my recording, although it's difficult to say. Can we identify them, Frank?'

'I doubt it as they've got their hoods up,' Frank said. 'We don't even know if they're boys or girls.'

'They walk like boys,' Whitney said.

'I agree,' George said as she followed Whitney back to the board. 'Attention, everyone. We've got a couple of suspicious young males who we can't identify. We need to come up with a way of getting them, or for someone they know, to come forward. Any ideas?'

'I have one,' Ellie said.

'Go on,' Whitney said.

'We can use social media. Put up a post offering a reward for information about the fires.'

George nodded, in approval. It was an excellent idea.

'It could work, but it will mean we'll be inundated with a huge number of false statements from people hoping to cash in. Providing everyone accepts that we'll be spending several days operating on caffeine and very little sleep, I'll run it past the super as we require his permission to offer a reward.'

'I'm up for it,' Doug said.

'Me, too,' Frank said.

Matt and Sue also agreed.

'PR will need to be involved. Remember, not everyone goes on social media, so we'll hold a press conference to inform the public. We'll also involve the schools in the area which means it's best if we coordinate everything for Monday.'

'I won't be around during the day on Monday as I'm back at work and have meetings,' George said.

'No problem, I'll text you and let you know how it goes.'

'I'm going home now if you no longer need me, as I'm going out later.'

'Okay. Thanks for your help. I'm off to see Jamieson, that's if he's in today.'

George watched as Whitney hastily exited the room, her whole demeanour invigorated. That's what was needed for them to catch the offenders.

TWENTY-SEVEN

Saturday 26 September

Before Whitney could get to Jamieson's office he appeared in the hallway. Lately he'd hardly been in his office as she always seemed to be meeting him outside of it.

'Sir, I was coming to see you.'

'What is it, Walker? I'm on my way out and don't have much time.'

'We've identified two teenage boys who we believe were hanging around near two of the fire sites. We'd like to offer a reward for information, to entice them out of the woodwork, or at least hear from someone who knows them. We're aware we'll have to deal with a number of tyre kickers, but the team are prepared for that.'

'The case needs solving, so if you believe this is the best course of action then I'll agree to it. What level of reward were you thinking of?'

She looked at him, surprised he was asking her opinion.

'I'm assuming it has to come out of the budget. What do you

suggest, sir?' she asked throwing it back at him, as she had no idea what he would deem appropriate.

'It has to be worthwhile. We'll offer twenty thousand pounds. We have a fund for such things.'

'Thanks. We'll arrange to make the announcement on Monday, early afternoon if possible. I want a three-pronged attack. Social media, the press, and schools.'

'Leave that to me. I'll make sure to be around then.'

'Thanks, sir.'

'Let's hope it's successful,' he said, striding past her.

She followed him down the stairs and returned to the incident room.

'Jamieson has agreed for us to offer a reward of twenty thousand pounds. Ellie, I want you to liaise with the PR department for putting it up on social media.'

'Yes, guv.'

'We'll let the press know on Monday which will capture the attention of the adults. Matt, arrange for uniformed officers to visit all of the schools in the area to inform the pupils of the reward.'

'When do you want them to visit?' Matt asked.

'I'd like us to coordinate everything to take place early afternoon on Monday. I'll let PR know. It might be more effective to bombard people with it, rather than spread it out. The hope is that we get a variety of people, from young to old, talking about the fires and the reward. Frank, download some images of the suspects so they can be taken to the schools. We'll also ask Melissa to circulate them to the media. Although *we* can't identify the boys, someone who knows them well might be able to work out who they are, by the way they walk and what they're wearing.'

'I'm onto it, guv,' the older officer said as he turned back to his computer while Ellie reached for the phone. Next to her Matt was busy texting.

Tears formed in her eyes and she quickly blinked them away. This could be the last case they worked on together. She didn't want them witnessing her losing it, so she turned and returned to her office, where she forced herself to do some of the admin that had been building up.

TWENTY-EIGHT

Monday, 28 September

Whitney followed Melissa and Jamieson into the meeting room to address the media. This was going to be make or break as everything hinged on the enticement of the reward. She'd spent yesterday ensuring everything was in order so that their plan would achieve maximum impact.

As usual, the room was full of reporters eager for the next instalment. On her less charitable days, she thought of them as vultures. At other times she accepted that they were just doing their job. And, to be fair, because she'd known most of them for many years, they had a mutual respect for one another.

After Melissa's introduction, Jamieson took the mic. 'As you are all aware, we've recently had four fires, resulting in the deaths of twenty-seven people. Fifty-two people were taken to the hospital, ten of whom were admitted. After extensive investigation, we're focusing our attention on tracking down two young males who were seen in the vicinity of two of the fires. Melissa will be sending you all a copy of their images from our CCTV footage. We are asking for anybody who recognises them, or knows anything in relation to the fires, to please come forward. There is a reward for any information that leads to the arrest of the person, or persons, responsible.'

'Are you saying that these two young men are the culprits?' a reporter towards the back of the room called out.

'No, that's not what we're claiming. I'll pass you over to Chief Inspector Walker and she'll give you more details.' He slid the mic over to her.

She suppressed a grin. In all the time she'd known Jamieson there had only been one occasion when he was prepared to field the difficult questions. That was when he was up for a promotion ... which he didn't get.

'I would like to confirm what Detective Superintendent Jamieson has said. We are not accusing these two young people of being responsible for the fires. We wish to find out who they are so we can interview them regarding anything they might have observed while being close to the sites, and also to eliminate them from our enquiries.'

'But you're not excluding them as suspects,' the reporter pushed.

'We follow all lines of enquiry, part of which is to interview anyone who might have information that will help,' Whitney said, fobbing him off. 'I repeat, if anybody has any information please come forward, however small or inconsequential it might seem.'

'How much is the reward?' a voice from the front row called out.

'We are offering twenty thousand pounds for anyone giving us information leading to a successful prosecution. These fires have to stop. We can't continue losing lives like this. All calls will be treated in confidence. That's all for now. Thank you very much for coming in.'

Whitney picked up her files and followed Melissa and Jamieson out of the room.

'Let's hope this jogs people's memories,' Jamieson said.

'I suspect we're going to be inundated with calls. I'll have officers on the phone for the rest of the day and throughout the night as when a reward is offered it does bring everybody out of the woodwork. But it's worth it if we get information leading us to the culprits.'

'Keep me informed. I won't be available in the morning as I'm having my interview.'

She glanced at him. He didn't appear worried, if anything his face was relaxed.

'Good luck, sir.'

'I don't need luck. It's more important that I make the correct decision regarding my future. There are plenty of opportunities out there for me.'

TWENTY-NINE

Monday, 28 September

It was almost five-thirty before George managed to get to the station. She'd had several back-to-back meetings during the day in preparation for the start of the new academic year, which had gone on for hours, as academics seemed unable to be concise about anything and, given the opportunity, would debate the number of angels that can dance on the head of a pin.

She found Whitney in her office.

'What are you doing here?' the officer said, glancing up at her, looking surprised.

'I thought I'd call in after work to see how it's all going as I haven't heard from you. Did the press conference turn up any new information?'

She'd been concerned that the pressure was mounting as Whitney was not only struggling with the uncertainty of her, and her team's, future, but also with their inability to solve the case thus far. George wanted to be there for her.

'Despite it only airing a few hours ago, we've been inundated with calls but, so far, we haven't identified the young men. Plenty of names have been suggested, and the team are working their arses off tracking them all down.'

'Give it time. It's hard for someone to come forward and give up someone they know. There's a process involved where they will want to consider the rights and wrongs of doing so.'

Whitney was distracted and George turned to see what had captured her attention.

Matt was marching towards them and she opened the door for him to come through.

'I think we might have something, guv. I've just come off the phone to a Mrs Hibbert. She believes her son could be involved.'

'What do we know about her?'

'She works in an office not far from here. She's calling in to see us on her way home. She won't be long.'

'George and I will go down to see her. I know you want to get off early to be with Leigh.'

'Thanks, guv. I appreciate it. I hope it doesn't cause an issue with the rest of the team.'

'They won't mind, I can assure you of that. You've more than pulled your weight. Off you go and I'll see you tomorrow.'

'Thanks, guv,' he said as he turned and headed out of the office.

Ten minutes later, a call came through to say that Mrs Hibbert was at the front desk and Whitney asked the sergeant to take her to one of the interview rooms.

George followed Whitney into the room, her eyes drawn to Mrs Hibbert, who was seated, her hands clasped together in her lap. She wore a black wool coat, which she hadn't undone despite it not being cold, with a pink scarf tied around her neck.

'Thank you for coming in,' Whitney said. 'Do you mind if I record this?'

Mrs Hibbert bit down on her bottom lip for a second. 'If that's what you have to do, then okay,' she said, nodding.

'It saves writing notes,' Whitney explained as she leant in front of George and pressed the button on the recording equipment. 'Interview on the twenty-eighth of September. Those present: Detective Chief Inspector Walker, Dr Cavendish and ... please could you state your name.'

'Beverley Hibbert.'

'I understand from my sergeant that you're concerned your son might be involved in the recent spate of fires,' Whitney said.

'Yes. I wasn't sure about coming forward, but so many people have died or been hurt. Once I saw the images of those boys, I suspected it was Alfie. I'm having such trouble with him. It's just the two of us at home, now his brother isn't living there. He's always been a handful, but as he's got older, he's got worse.'

'Could you explain in what way?' Whitney asked.

'A few weeks ago, I found him and his friend in the garden setting fire to some textbooks from school. I watched for a while before confronting them. Alfie stared at the flames like they were hypnotising him. When I finally went up to them to ask why they were burning them, Alfie said they were from last year, so he didn't need them.'

'Was this the first time you'd witnessed him having a fascination with fire?' George asked.

'Yes, but for a long time I've thought something wasn't right. Sometimes his clothes smell of smoke, and I've found burn holes when washing them. When I asked him about it, he said he didn't know how it happened. There have also been burn marks in the carpet, which he denied all knowledge of.'

'How old is your son?' Whitney asked.

'He's fifteen.'

'You said he was with another boy. Do you know him well?' Whitney asked.

'His name is Jay Walton, and they're always together. He's much quieter than Alfie, though.'

'Would you say that your son is the leader out of the two of them?' George asked.

'Yes. He does seem to instigate what they do. He's been caught shoplifting before but got a warning. I don't know what to do with him. I want to believe it's not him, but everything points to it.' She bowed her head.

'Where is your son at the moment?'

'He's at our house with Jay. He phoned while I was at work to say where they were, and that Jay was going to stay for dinner.'

'So, he does keep in touch to let you know what's going on?' Whitney said.

'If he does, it's to ask for something. He won't bother phoning otherwise. Today it was because he wanted some money. I expect he rummaged through my pockets and drawers in search of some before calling. I've learnt the hard way not to keep money in the house as it goes missing.'

This could be the break Whitney had been hoping for. The evidence had suggested to George that their culprit would be young, but fifteen-year-olds being responsible for all those deaths ...

'I'd like you to go home as usual so the boys don't suspect anything,' Whitney said. 'I'll be at your house soon and bring officers with me. Please don't warn them.'

'You must think I'm a really bad parent for dropping my son in it. But what else could I do?' A single tear slid down her cheek.

'You've done the right thing,' Whitney said, sliding the box of tissues over to the woman. 'I know it's hard, but he obviously needs some help. We'll sort this out, I promise.'

'Will he go to prison?'

'If the evidence suggests he's the person responsible, or he admits it, he'll be charged and go through the youth courts. If found guilty, he'll most likely be sent to a young offender institution. But we're jumping the gun. First, we need to speak to Alfie and Jay. Thank you for coming in. We appreciate how difficult it's been for you.'

'That's an understatement,' the woman said, shaking her head.

'Do you have a photo of Alfie?' Whitney asked.

'On my phone.' She pulled out her phone and showed it to Whitney.

'Please will you forward it to me, here's my number.' Whitney handed the woman her card.

After Mrs Hibbert had sent the photo she was shown out of the station and Whitney and George returned to the incident room. Whitney wrote the names of the two boys on the board.

She called everyone to attention. 'I think we've got the names of the two boys that we've been looking for. Alfie Hibbert and Jay Walton. We've been speaking to the mother of the ring-leader, Alfie. She's convinced her son might be mixed up in all this as he has a fascination with fire and is out of control. She doesn't trust him.'

'She's dropping her son in it for murder. Strange how she only came forward once a reward was offered. What sort of parent does that?' Frank said, his bottom lip curling.

'Frank, cool it. She was alerted after seeing images of the boys and the reward wasn't even mentioned. She's a distraught mother, but she also has a responsibility to those who have been killed. Instead of criticising, you should be praising her,' Whitney said.

'It would have been extremely hard for her to come and speak to us,' George said.

'Exactly,' Whitney said. 'However much she loves her son, she knew she had to do what's right.'

'Sorry, guv,' Frank said.

'We're getting sidetracked. We know both boys are at the Hibbert house in Byron Road right now. Before we bring them in for questioning, I'm going to visit the house of Jay Walton to speak to his parents and let them know what's happening, as he's underage.'

'Is going there first wise, guv?' Frank asked.

'I have no reason to believe they're a flight risk. Mrs Hibbert is on her way home and as Alfie has already informed her that Jay will be there for dinner, it points to them not planning to go anywhere until after they've eaten. I'm going to call Matt and ask him to come back in.' Whitney pulled out her phone and keyed in a number. 'Sorry, Matt, I need you back here straight away.'

'Do you need me?' George asked, once Whitney had ended her call. She'd already made plans to see Ross.

'Not on the operation, in case it doesn't go as planned. But it will be useful if you can observe the interviews when we're back here.'

'When will that be?'

'I'm not sure. Do you have plans?'

'Well ...' George hesitated.

'Are you going out with Ross?' Whitney said, quietly.

'I'd made an arrangement with him, but—'

'We can manage without you, if you want to go,' Whitney said, interrupting her.

'No. I'd rather be here to watch the interviews.' Whitney needed her. Ross would understand.

'Okay, thanks,' Whitney said. 'Right, let's finalise our plan. Matt and I will go to the Waltons' and then to Byron Street. Doug, take Sue and meet us there. We'll then have two cars and take one boy in each.'

'Yes, guv,' Doug said.

'Ellie, I want you to look into both boys. Check their social media accounts, and those of their friends. Look for anything which might help us. It's important to check if there's any gang connection. We also need to know if there are more than the two of them involved. I'll forward you a photo of Alfie if you could please send it to everyone? Also, find a photo of Jay Walton and send that.'

'Yes, guv,' Ellie said.

'Can you manage without me?' Frank asked.

George glanced at the officer who couldn't quite meet Whitney's eyes. As loyal as he was to Whitney, he did often push things.

'Have you got somewhere to go?' Whitney asked.

'I've promised to take the wife out for dinner this evening if it was possible to leave early,' Frank said.

'Is it a special occasion?' Whitney asked.

'Not really, she just said she didn't fancy cooking.'

'Didn't you warn her that we'd be working all hours once the reward was offered?'

'No, in case she went off on one. You know what she's like.'

'I need you on the operation, so let her know that you won't be taking her out.'

'Doing what? You hadn't included me up to now.'

'You're staying here with Ellie, answering the phones.'

'Can I go once you're back?' he asked.

Whitney exchanged a glance with George and rolled her eyes. 'If it all runs smoothly, then yes, you can leave after we have both boys back at the station, providing the others don't mind taking the calls in your absence as there will still be plenty coming in.'

'Guys?' Frank pleaded.

'I don't mind,' Ellie said.

'Me neither,' said Doug.

'Thanks, guv. I'll tell the wife we'll be leaving later than planned.'

Whitney turned to George. 'Are you going to wait here, or go home?'

'I'll wait here and do some work. It's pointless going all the way home just to come back later.'

'Fine. There are plenty of spare desks. I'm going to wait in here for Matt, then go.' Whitney turned to the rest of the team. 'Okay, this is it. I can feel it in my stomach. These boys are our arsonists, so let's go and get them.'

THIRTY

Monday, 28 September

Whitney and Matt drove to a housing estate on the east side of Lenchester. It was an area she knew well from when she was on the beat as they were often being called out there.

They drove up to a small terraced house dating back to the 1980s and parked outside. The house was well kept, with a small front lawn and an attractive flower border around the edge. They walked up the short path and she rang the bell.

'Leave the talking to me,' she said to Matt.

'Yes, guv, I know,' he said, giving a wry grin.

After a short while, the door was opened by a woman wearing a uniform from one of the local supermarkets.

'Are you the parent of Jay Walton?' Whitney asked.

'Yes, I'm Cerys Walton. Why?' the woman replied, her eyes darting from Whitney to Matt.

'I'm Detective Chief Inspector Walker and this is Detective Sergeant Price. We'd like to come in for a moment, please?'

'What's it about? What's happened? What's he done? Has

he been in trouble? Has there been an accident?' The words spilled out of her mouth.

'It's okay, he's not hurt,' Whitney said, wanting to reassure her. 'We'd like to speak to you inside, if we may.'

The woman breathed an audible sigh of relief as she opened the door for them to walk in. The entrance led straight into a lounge which was clean and comfortably furnished, although the furniture was dated. There was a dark red sofa and two chairs at the front of the room overlooking the road, and at the back a circular dark wood dining table with four matching chairs.

'Come in and sit down,' Cerys Walton said, gesturing to the sofa.

'Are you alone?' Whitney asked.

'My daughter's upstairs on her computer. You know what teenagers are like, you can't get them away from their screens.' She gave a laugh which appeared tinged with guilt.

'Who lives here?' Whitney asked.

'There are the four of us. Jay, Jade, and my husband, Rich. He's at work at the moment. Please tell me why you're here.'

'I'm very sorry to tell you, but we have reason to believe that your son might have been involved in some incidents with Alfie Hibbert.'

'That boy,' she said. 'He's trouble, with a capital T. I don't know why Jay has to hang around with him. My Jay used to be such a good boy. He always did his homework on time and parents' evenings were a pleasure. Now, it's all changed. We've been called into school so often. He's fine when he's on his own but as soon as he's with Alfie … it's like the boy has some magical hold over Jay. What trouble have they got into?'

'You may have heard about the recent series of fires we've had in the area.'

A hand flew to her mouth. 'No, surely not. You can't think that he would do that. People have died in those fires. He's a good boy underneath it all. He'd never do anything like that, I'm sure of it.'

'You may have seen on the news that we're tracing two young people, most likely male, who seemed to be around the age of the two boys. Following our appeal, a witness has come forward naming Alfie and Jay. We're not saying they are responsible, but we do need to speak to them.'

'I can't believe it. No way would Jay ever be involved in something like this. You've got it wrong. I'm sure you have.'

'At the moment we just want to speak to the boys, and eliminate them from our enquiries,' Whitney said in an attempt to pacify her.

'I'll have to contact my husband at work and let him know. He'll agree with me, I know he will. Even if Alfie did it, Jay wouldn't have. He's a good boy.'

'The boys are currently at Alfie's house and we're going to interview them at the station after we've collected them from there.'

'Can I come with you?'

'You can meet us at the station but please don't contact Jay as we don't want to alarm the boys in case they attempt something stupid, like running away.'

'I won't say anything other than asking my husband to meet us so we can both be there for Jay.'

'Where does he work?'

'In the warehouse at Turner's Auto Parts. Can we both be with Jay during the interview?'

'Only one of you will be allowed in,' Whitney said.

'I'll speak to my husband and we'll decide. I can't believe they're both involved, surely it's going to be a misunderstanding.'

'Once we've spoken to the boys we'll find out,' Whitney said.

They left the house and returned to the car.

'Do you think it was wise leaving her?' Matt asked.

'I don't think she'll warn him. We're literally going around the corner so let's hope she won't,' she said, suddenly doubting what she'd done.

They drove to Byron Road and parked outside the Hibbert house. It was similar in style to the one they'd left, only this one was an end of terrace and had a bigger garden which wrapped around the side of the house. They parked in front of Doug's car.

'All set?' she asked Doug when she reached his car.

'Yes, guv.'

'Matt and I will go in and talk to the boys and bring them out. You and Sue stand by the gate while we're in there, in case the boys make a dash for it, though I doubt they will.'

Before they'd even reached the front door, it opened, and Mrs Hibbert stood there, her mouth set in a fine line.

'I was expecting you sooner,' she said, shifting awkwardly from foot to foot.

'We went to the Waltons' house. They're going to meet us at the station. I assume you're going to be there, too?'

'Of course,' Mrs Hibbert said.

'We are going to take the two boys in separate cars,' Whitney said.

'Are you going to arrest them and take them out in handcuffs?'

'No, nothing like that,' Whitney said. 'We'll ask them to come down to the station with us and keep it very low-key.'

'Thank you. I don't want the neighbours to see what's going on.'

'May we come inside? I'm sure you don't want to have this conversation on the doorstep.'

'Sorry, I wasn't thinking.' She stepped to the side and they walked in.

'Have you mentioned anything to the boys?' Whitney asked.

'No. You asked me not to,' she said.

'Good. Where are they now?'

'Upstairs in Alfie's room. They haven't come out of there since I arrived home.'

'You mentioned Alfie has an older brother, do you want to contact him for support?'

'No. I haven't seen Stevie for a long time. I asked him to leave because he'd joined a gang and I didn't want Alfie to be influenced by them.'

Whitney went on full alert.

'Do you know the name of the gang?'

'Yes, he belongs to the *Lenchester Reds.*'

She glanced at Matt, who was nodding. This case was about to blow wide open.

'Is Alfie's father around?'

'He died when Alfie was seven. If he was here, we wouldn't be having these problems. I tried my best, but he's out of control. If he did those awful things, it's all my fault ...'

'Let's just take it one step at a time,' Whitney said, resting a hand on the woman's arm.

Her son may have been responsible for the deaths of all those people, but that didn't mean she was to blame.

'Would you like me to call them down or shall I take you up to Alfie's bedroom?'

'We'll go to his bedroom in case they decide to run away,' Whitney said. 'Do you think that's likely?'

'Your guess is as good as mine,' Mrs Hibbert said, letting out a resigned sigh. 'Follow me.'

When they reached the top of the stairs, Mrs Hibbert stopped outside the second door on the left. She knocked and opened it.

'What do you want? I've told you not to come in without

being asked.' The angry tone in the boy's voice shocked Whitney. Thank goodness Tiffany had never been like that.

'There's someone here to see you,' Mrs Hibbert said, her face bright red.

Whitney and Matt stepped forward and walked into the room at the same time as Alfie and the other boy turned around.

'I'm Detective Chief Inspector Walker and this is Detective Sergeant Price. We're here to talk to both of you about the fires we've had recently in Lenchester.'

The two boys looked at each other, but while Alfie's expression remained unchanged, Jay's eyes widened, and his nostrils flared.

'It's nothing to do with us,' Alfie said, crossing his arms and staring directly at them, his eyes mocking.

'We're going to take you both down to the station for an interview,' Whitney said, flatly.

'Why? We didn't do anything,' Alfie said.

'You were both seen in the vicinity of two fires. Jay, your parents are going to meet us there.'

'You've spoken to them?' Jay said, colour draining from his face.

'Yes. One of them will be with you during the interview.'

'I keep telling you, it's nothing to do with us,' Alfie said.

'We can discuss all this at the station.'

'Are you arresting us?' Alfie asked.

'No. We're inviting you to come of your own accord but if you refuse, you will be arrested.'

Both boys followed them downstairs.

'Alfie, you and your mother are coming with me and Detective Sergeant Price. Jay, you're going with officers waiting outside.'

'Why can't we all go together?' Alfie asked.

'There isn't room,' Whitney said, in her no-nonsense voice.

'I'm not going then.' He scowled at Whitney.

'I suggest you make this easy on yourself,' she replied in a low, cold voice. 'Because if you don't come voluntarily you will be taken out of here in handcuffs under arrest.'

'I don't care.' He shrugged.

'Think of your mother and what this is doing to her,' Whitney growled, sharper than she'd intended, but the little shit was getting to her.

He looked at his mum and gave a grunt. 'Okay, I'll go with you.'

Doug was waiting by the front door and escorted Jay to his car while Whitney and Matt took Alfie and his mother.

THIRTY-ONE

Monday, 28 September

George sat in Whitney's office, away from the others, and pulled out her phone to call Ross.

'Hello, George,' he said, answering almost immediately.

'You haven't left yet, have you?' she asked.

They'd planned to go out for a meal in a pub close to where George lived, which meant he had a fifty-minute drive.

'I was about to. Is everything still okay for this evening?'

'I'm sorry to give you such short notice, but I need to be here at the station with Whitney. She wants me to observe some interviews. The suspects aren't here yet, and I've no idea how long it will take.'

'Are they involved with the arson cases?'

George bristled. She had mentioned that's what they were working on and knew he wouldn't say anything, but it still made her uneasy. Not that she'd ever told him anything confidential. She knew better than to do that. As usual she was overthinking. She really needed to *lighten up*, as Whitney would say.

'Yes, that's correct.'

'They've arrested someone?'

'You know better than to ask me that,' she snapped.

He laughed. 'Don't worry, George, I don't have a hotline to the media. I totally understand about the confidential aspect of your work with the police.'

'I'm sorry, my tone was uncalled for,' George said.

'Apology accepted. What time do you think you'll be free? Is it worth me still coming over? It doesn't matter how late. We can meet at your house.'

Although neither of them had voiced it in so many words, it seemed they were officially back in a relationship. She'd persuaded herself to not overthink it and to be far more laissez-faire in her approach. Whitney, no doubt, would find that amusing.

'I've no idea how long these interviews are going to last. It's possible they may go through the night, so I think it's best if we call off tonight.'

She didn't want to have one eye on the suspects and the other on the clock, worrying about keeping Ross waiting. This was a much better plan.

'I understand. What about tomorrow, shall we go out then?'

'Let's wait and see what happens regarding the case.' She didn't want to commit to anything and then have to let him down again.

'Okay, why don't you get in touch if you're free at all during the week. Do you have anything planned for the weekend?'

'Not at the moment.'

'There's an exhibit of ancient Egyptian artefacts in Huddersfield if you fancy going?'

She'd actually seen it advertised and thought it would be very interesting.

'I'd love to go. From what I've read about it, it will be fascinating.'

'Great.' She could hear the smile in his voice. 'We'll make a weekend of it. We'll drive up first thing Saturday morning and stay overnight, if that's okay with you?'

'Yes, I'd like that very much.'

'I'll book us a hotel room.'

'I'm sorry about cancelling tonight.'

'It's fine, I know Whitney comes first.'

Is that what he thought?

'She doesn't, as a rule of thumb, but we're at a crucial point in the case, as I've already explained. We have to be mindful of the fact that we may not have the guilty parties in custody and, if that's the case, we have to do what we can to stop further deaths occurring. That's what takes precedence.'

'I was joking,' he said.

'I know that,' she lied, not wanting to admit how she'd misinterpreted him.

'I totally understand the importance of what you're doing.'

'Thank you. I'll see you Saturday, if not before.'

She ended the call, the tightness in her neck gone. She'd forgotten how much she'd enjoyed their conversations. Thank goodness she was able to rectify her mistake of ending it between them.

She glanced up and saw Whitney heading towards her.

'Do you want my job?' the officer asked as she stood in the doorway, grinning.

'No. Why do you think that?'

'Sitting in my chair,' Whitney replied, laughing. 'You know you'd have to deal with Jamieson and all the other shit that comes my way.'

'I came in here to use my phone so I couldn't be overhead.'

'Let me guess, you were speaking to Ross?'

'How do you know?'

'Who else would it be?'

'I cancelled our engagement this evening.'

'You didn't have to.'

'I did. You need me here to observe. He didn't mind, and we've just arranged to go to Huddersfield to an exhibition on Saturday and stay overnight. It will be a pleasant weekend.'

'I'm so happy that you're back together,' Whitney said. 'I'm assuming you are, even though you haven't actually told me.'

'Yes, you're correct, we have resumed our relationship, which I'm very happy about.'

'My goodness, you're actually admitting something to do with your feelings. That's got to be a first,' Whitney said, smirking.

'I don't know what you mean.' George let out an exasperated sigh.

'Never mind, I'm only poking fun. Down to business. We've got the boys downstairs and, more importantly, we've learnt from Mrs Hibbert that Alfie's brother is in the *Lenchester Reds*. We have our link.'

'If he's the one setting the fires, it could be to impress his brother. Or the gang. It could be some sort of initiation. Though from my reading of gang behaviour, causing a substantial number of deaths over a period of time isn't something required of new members. Acid attacks are often carried out on innocent people, as is torture and stabbing of the person wanting to enter the gang. But multiple fires? It's a new one on me.'

'Do you believe this is something he's decided to do for himself, not directed by the gang?' Whitney asked, leaning against the door frame with her arms folded.

'It's certainly a line you need to follow. Who are you interviewing first?' she asked.

'Alfie as he's the leader of the two. Then we'll speak to Jay.'

'You should consider the other way around. The weaker one might crack first,' George suggested.

'I had thought about that, but I think he'll be too scared to speak. I'm hoping that when we interview Alfie, he'll let something useful slip, especially if he's trying to show off, as we all know fifteen-year-old boys are prone to do. Then we can use the information he gives us when interviewing Jay. We'll give the impression we know more than we do.'

'That does seem a good plan,' George acknowledged. 'Don't start with the gang link. Lead up to it. Let him believe you're only discussing the fires and then drop it in. It will give me a chance to set a baseline for his answers and then I can note any changes in his demeanour.'

After collecting Matt, they went downstairs to the interview room where Alfie Hibbert was situated.

George entered the observation room and looked through at Mrs Hibbert sitting next to her son. Her face was pinched, and worry lines accentuated her eyes. Her hands were clenched and resting on the table. By contrast, Alfie, who had very similar features to his mother, with the same oval-shaped face and angular jaw, was lounging in the chair with one arm resting over the back. He was acting like he hadn't got a care in the world. Was it all bravado? It would be interesting to see how it played out.

As Whitney and Matt entered, the woman sat even more upright, but the boy didn't even bother to look at them. He kept staring to the side. The interview wasn't going to be easy for Whitney. He was only fifteen, yet seemed to have no concern for the situation he was in. What had happened for him to become like that?

Whitney pressed the button on the recording equipment.

'Interview on September the twenty-eighth. Those present: Detective Chief Inspector Walker and Detective Sergeant Price.' Whitney looked at the woman. 'Please state your name for the recording.'

'Beverley Hibbert,' she said.

Whitney's head turned in the direction of the boy. He glanced up and made eye contact.

'Please state your name for the recording,' Whitney said.

He didn't say a thing. His mother looked at him.

'Just say your name. You're in enough trouble as it is,' Mrs Hibbert said.

He gave a shrug. 'Alfie Hibbert.'

'I'd like to talk to you about where you've been on the evenings when there have been fires in the city.' Whitney opened the file she'd placed on the table and took out a copy of the CCTV footage image and slid it over. 'Is this you?'

He glanced down at the photo and then averted his gaze.

'Answer the officer,' his mum said, nudging him with her elbow.

'Ouch. What did you do that for?' he said, scowling at his mother and rubbing his arm.

'Is this you and Jay Walton?' Whitney repeated.

The boy shrugged. 'It might have been.'

'This image was captured half an hour before the fire in Wellington Street. What were you doing there?'

'We were out walking.'

'At that time of night?' she said.

'I'm not a baby. I don't have a curfew. If I want to be out, then I can.'

Whitney took out two more photos from the file, captured from the videos on her phone. 'Is *this* you and Jay Walton?' She pointed to the shadows.

He pulled them closer and stared at them. 'I don't know, it might have been.'

'This was taken while the fire service was dealing with the fire at the factory in Brook Street. Did you watch the fire?' Whitney pushed.

'Maybe.'

'Ask him how he felt observing the fires,' George said.

Whitney gave an acknowledging nod.

'When you're watching a fire, how does it make you feel? Does it get you excited? Or does it scare you? Do you want to get as close as possible to the flames?' Whitney asked, leaning towards him slightly.

'I didn't feel anything. I was just watching, the same as all of the other people there.'

'Why didn't you come forward when we asked for anybody who had any information regarding the fires?'

'Because I didn't have any. We happened to be passing, saw the fire engines and watched. It's not a crime, you know.'

George studied his face. It was the most he'd spoken. 'His eyes became alert and bright when he was talking about the incident. He definitely knows more than he's letting on. Keep asking him about fire and what it means to him.'

'Do you like fire? When you see the flames, does it give you a thrill? Lots of people are fascinated by fire,' Whitney asked.

'What do you mean, do I *like* it? That's like asking if I like chocolate.'

George nodded. He certainly didn't fit into the low IQ category. If he was tested, she wouldn't be surprised if his score was above average.

'Did you have anything to do with starting these fires?' Whitney asked.

'No, I didn't. Just because I was seen close by, you can't pin them on me. I know what you lot are like, trying to find someone to fit up to help your clear-up rate.'

'How do you know *what we're like?*' Whitney asked using quote marks with her fingers. 'Don't you think it's a bit of a coincidence that you were close to all of them?' Whitney asked.

George cringed at Whitney's use of the word coincidence, though she suspected the officer did it because she knew it frustrated her. It was Whitney's idea of fun.

'Why don't you listen? Jay and me ... we just happened to be there.'

'At every fire?'

'Not *every* one,'

'But you didn't come forward when we put out an appeal. Instead we had to find you. I'm sure you can see how that looks.'

'I knew you'd try to pin it on us, that's why we kept away. But we didn't do anything.' He looked at his mother. 'Honest, Mum, we didn't do anything. We were just there ... You've got to believe me.'

'Let's go back to the fire in Stanton Road on September thirteenth. What time did you go out that night and where did you go to?'

'I can't remember when we went out, maybe around seven. We just hung around the streets, like we usually do.'

'What time did you get back?'

'I can't remember, but it wasn't late.' He shook his head.

Mrs Hibbert stared at her son, disbelief in her eyes.

'It's a lie,' George said. 'I can see it in his mother's eyes.'

'Try harder, Alfie, because I think you're lying to me. Now tell me again, what time did you arrive home on September the thirteenth?'

'I don't remember.' He sat back in his chair, his arms folded tightly across his chest.

'You're trying my patience,' Whitney said sharply. 'I want a straight answer. Were you in the vicinity of the first fire in Stanton Road at around midnight when it was blazing?'

'I can't remember but I definitely had nothing to do with starting the fires.'

'You're going around in circles,' George said. 'I suggest you leave that avenue now and ask him about the gang.'

Whitney took out the photo of the garden gnome wearing the bandana and slid it over to him.

'Recognise this?' she asked.

He leant forward and gave it a cursory glance. 'No.'

'He's lying. His body tensed and his eyes flickered in recognition when you showed it to him.'

'What about the bandana tied around the gnome? Surely you recognise it?'

He moved awkwardly in his seat. 'No.'

'Tell me about your brother Stevie. Is it right that your mum asked him to leave home because he was a member of the *Lenchester Reds?*'

'What did you tell them that for?' he said, glaring at his mother. She bowed her head and turned from him.

'The bandana that had been tied around the gnome is theirs, isn't it?'

'If you say so.'

'Do you know where we found it?' Whitney asked. 'Well, I'll tell you. It was in the garden of the house in Rushmere Close which was set on fire. The one where a mother and her two children died. Were you close to that fire when it was blazing?'

'I don't remember.'

'What do you think the gnome and bandana signify?'

'Ask them. It was nothing to do with me.'

'His tone is less certain than before. My advice is to leave him for a while to ponder on what you know, and what's going to happen next,' George said.

'This interview is suspended for the time being. We'll be back to see you again shortly,' Whitney said, as she stopped the recording and picked up her folders from the table.

'I want to go home,' Alfie said.

'We can't allow you to, yet,' Whitney said.

'Are you arresting me?'

'No, we're not, but if you do attempt to leave, then we will.'

'Just behave yourself,' Mrs Hibbert said to her son, as Whitney and Matt left the room.

THIRTY-TWO

Monday, 28 September

George walked into the corridor at the same time as Matt and Whitney left the interview room.

'Thanks for the input. What were your overall conclusions?' Whitney asked her.

'As soon as you mentioned the fire, he changed quite noticeably.'

'He appeared the same to me throughout the interview. A belligerent little shit, who needed taking in hand,' Matt said.

'That's because George is the expert, and you're not.' Whitney nudged him.

'There were marked differences in his behaviour as the interview progressed,' George said. 'Most notably in his eyes. They became alert and focused, as he went back to the memory of the fires he'd witnessed.'

'I can't believe you got all that from his behaviour, it's incredible,' Matt said.

'It was the mention of the gang that made him uneasy as he hadn't banked on you establishing a link,' George said.

'That's ridiculous. Why leave the gnome with a bandana if it wasn't to make the gang participation known?'

'He's fifteen and for all his bravado and intelligence, hadn't thought it through.'

'Luckily for us, as without it we might not have got this far,' Whitney said. 'Did he seem worried or concerned that he was being interviewed?'

'For the most part, no. If anything, he enjoyed the attention as he's convinced himself you won't be able to pin it on him.'

'At his age, it could be he hasn't understood the severity of the situation he's in,' Whitney said.

'He's a very intelligent young man, unlike many arsonists of his age. If anything, he believes he's too clever to be caught.'

'Even though we know about the gang?'

'That's the one area which concerned him, but not enough for him to admit to everything.'

'Thanks, George. Let's interview Jay Walton and see if we can get anything from him. All we know so far is that he's the quiet one and, according to his mother, he's under the influence of Alfie. We might get something from him now, especially as Alfie has admitted they were there. I'll embellish that slightly which might persuade him to add more,' Whitney said.

'It will be interesting to see how he reacts,' George replied.

They walked together to the next interview room and George slipped into the observation area next door.

The young man sat there with his head bowed and his hands tightly balled in his lap. His dark fringe fell across his face. He seemed contrite from what she could see from his body language. There was an older man with him. His father? There was a resemblance.

Whitney and Matt entered, and the boy immediately sat upright and looked at them.

'Are you Mr Walton?' Whitney asked.

'Yes. We decided it was best if my wife stayed at home with our daughter,' he said.

Whitney pressed the recording equipment, made the statutory identifications of who was there, and started the interview.

'Jay, I'd like you to take a look at these photos.' She took them from the folder and slid them over to him, one at a time. 'We understand from Alfie that these are of both of you. Is that correct?'

'Yes,' the boy said.

'These put you both close to the fires in Stanton Road, Brook Street, and Wellington Street.'

'Yes.'

'How could you have been out at that time?' Mr Walton said.

'It was easy when I was staying at Alfie's because his mum goes to bed early. Once I crept out through the back door when you and Mum were both asleep in bed. I'm sorry.'

'We had no idea he'd been going out at night.' He glanced at Whitney and grimaced.

'I didn't do it very often,' Jay said. 'We mainly went out when I was staying overnight with Alfie.'

'So, you admit to being close to all three fires, I mentioned. What about the fire in Rushmere Close?'

'We were at all of them.'

'Ask him his feelings towards fire, to see if they coincide with Alfie's. I suspect they might not,' George said.

'How did you feel when you were looking at fires?'

'Scared. I was worried we might get burnt.'

'Were you and Alfie responsible for setting fires in Stanton Road, Brook Street, Rushmere Close, and Wellington Street?'

The boy tensed and he averted his eyes.

'Keep going. I think he's going to admit it,' George said.

'Tell the truth,' Mr Walton said, his voice gentler than before. 'It will be better in the long run.'

'I can't.' He shuddered.

'Yes, you can. I'm here to protect you,' Mr Walton said.

'You don't understand. Alfie ... he'll ... I just can't, Dad. Please don't make me.'

'Jay, twenty-seven people have died. Their families deserve to know what happened,' Whitney said.

'I didn't do it,' he said, looking at his dad.

'But you were there when Alfie started them?' Whitney asked. He nodded his head. 'Please speak for the recording.'

'Yes. I was.'

'Did you try to stop Alfie?' Whitney asked.

'I tried, but he wouldn't listen to me. We always have to do what he wants. He made me go with him and threatened to kill my whole family if I didn't. He said he'd set fire to our house when we were asleep. I didn't know if he was joking or not.' He turned to look at his father, who was clearly finding it hard to keep it together. 'I had to go with him, Dad. I couldn't risk it.' He let out a sob and his father pulled him into his arms. He appeared so much younger than fifteen.

'So many people killed,' Mr Walton muttered over the top of his son's head. 'So many ...'

Once Jay had calmed down, Whitney passed over to him the photo with the gnome and bandana. 'Have you seen this before?'

He glanced at his father, grimacing. 'Um ...'

'Go on, son,' his father said.

'Yes, I have,' he said softly.

'Do you know what the bandana signifies?'

'Yes. It's from the gang Alfie wants to join so he can be with his brother. That's why he set the fires, so they'd let him in.'

'Do you want to join as well?'

Mr Walton turned to his son. 'Over my dead body.'

'I don't want to, Dad.' Jay gave a vigorous shake of his head.

'Why were so many fires set? Was it his gang initiation test?' Whitney asked.

'No. They didn't tell him to do it. Alfie said he did it to impress the elders.'

'That doesn't answer the question about the bandana,' George said. 'There was something different about that fire.'

'I'd like to return to the fire in Rushmere Close. Why was a bandana left there, but not at any of the others?'

'Alfie said he did it for someone special, some woman.'

'Did he tell you the name of this woman?'

'He always called her C?'

'How does Alfie know her?'

'He met her sometimes when he went to the gang HQ to see his brother.'

'We believe she's the gang leader's sister, now known as Charlotte Payne. Did you ever go with him to meet her?' Whitney asked.

'No.'

'I hope you're telling the truth,' Mr Walton said.

'I am, Dad. I promise. Alfie said he wouldn't ever take me because I'd be too scared. I didn't want to go, anyway.'

'Jay, I want to ask you about setting the fires. Where did the petrol and cigarettes come from?'

'Alfie bought petrol from the garage and put it into a red plastic container that he got from home. He already had the cigs from his brother.'

'The fire inspector found two cigarette butts at each scene, did you smoke one of them?'

Silence hung in the air while Jay stared directly ahead.

'Jay?' his father said.

'Yes, but it was Alfie who pushed them through the letter box to set fire to the cloth covered in petrol he'd put through. It wasn't me, I promise.' A sob erupted from the boy and he shook.

'There's nothing in his body language to indicate he's lying.

His breathing and voice were steady, but I imagine it's going to be a case of *he said/he said*, after you speak to Alfie,' George said.

'Jay,' Whitney said, gently. 'When we interview Alfie, I suspect he's going to blame you, in the same way you're blaming him. If you're telling the truth, we need some evidence to back it up. Do you have anything?'

'What sort of evidence?' He looked helplessly at his father.

'Anything that might prove Alfie coerced you into coming along with him.'

He remained silent for a while until his eyes flickered. 'I've just remembered. I've got some messages on my phone, that Alfie sent me. They'll prove it wasn't me.'

'Get your phone out then,' Mr Walton said. 'Why didn't you tell us this before?'

'I forgot.' He took out his phone from his jacket pocket, opened it, and slid it over to Whitney. 'Here they are.'

'Read them out,' George said.

'*Alfie: You've got to come with me, I need you to record it. You'll enjoy it. You know you will.*

'*Me: I don't want to.*

'*Alfie: I've bought all the stuff. You don't have to do anything except hold up my phone.*

'*Me: I'm not sure.*

'*Alfie: You know what will happen if you don't.*'

'Now do you believe me?' Jay asked, relief in his voice.

'It's certainly going in your favour. I'll need to take your phone,' Whitney said, holding out her hand.

'I've just thought of something else. If you look at Alfie's phone, you'll see a video of him talking about the fires. He made me hold the camera while he recorded it.'

'How can you not have remembered all this before?' Mr Walton asked.

'I was scared.' He hung his head.

'We should have put a stop to this friendship in the first place but it's hard to interfere with teenage boys. Will Jay be charged?' A vein throbbed in Mr Walton's neck.

'It's up to the Crown Prosecution Service, but it's most likely that he will be charged as an accessory.'

'But I didn't do anything,' Jay said, sniffing.

'You were there, son, and you knew what was going on. I know you were scared but you could've come to me.'

'I advise you to contact a solicitor, or we can arrange one for you,' Whitney said.

'Will he be let out on bail?'

'We won't oppose it.'

They left the room and George met them in the corridor.

'Those messages confirm it's Alfie,' George said. 'Next steps?'

'We get him to confess.'

THIRTY-THREE

Monday, 28 September

Mixed emotions ran through Whitney as they returned to the interview room where they'd left Alfie Hibbert and his mum. She was relieved they'd solved the case and there would be no more fires. But they had two fifteen-year-old boys whose lives were going to be changed forever because of what they'd done. Not to mention all the families that had been torn apart. They deserved to be punished, but at this age, children were often unable to work out the consequences of their actions.

She left George in the observation room and went back in with Matt. The boy acted oblivious to her presence.

'Alfie, we have a few more questions,' Whitney said, after restarting the recording equipment. 'In our interview with Jay he admitted to being present when the fires were set but that you were the one who did it.'

His eyes blazed with anger. 'If he said that, he's lying to try to worm his way out of it. It was nothing to do with me. He was the one who did it. You can't blame me for the fires, they were his idea. I tried to stop him, but he wouldn't listen.'

'Why did you go with him, if you didn't want anything to do with it?' Whitney asked.

'Because he begged me to. He was just showing off.'

'If it was Jay, how do you account for the gang bandana being left at Rushmere Close?'

'Jay wants to be part of the *Lenchester Reds*. He's jealous that I know people in there.'

'Surely, if that was the reason, he would have left bandanas at all of the fires, but he didn't. Why not?'

'Ask him.' Alfie shrugged.

'Do you know Charlotte Payne?'

'Good question. You took him by surprise. He does know her, it's written all over his face,' George said.

'Who?' he said.

'Daz Hunt's sister.'

'I can't remember.'

'Charlotte Payne has been having an affair with the husband of the woman who died in the Rushmere Close fire. Did she ask you to set the fire to get his family out of the way?'

'I've already told you, Jay set the fires. Ask him.'

'We already have, and he has no knowledge of the woman, other than you referred to her as C. Stop messing us around and tell the truth.' Whitney drew in a breath. She hadn't intended to lose it.

'I am.'

'Alfie,' Mrs Hibbert said, 'tell the police what they want to know.'

'All I'm saying is that I was there, but it was Jay who lit those buildings on fire. I tried to stop him.'

'His mother doesn't believe him, but she won't admit it to you,' George said.

'Alfie, as I've already said, during our interview with Jay he admits to being there when the fires were set but said it was nothing to do with him. He said you started the fires and instigated everything. He also said you forced him to go with you.'

'You can't prove anything. It's his word against mine and I will never admit to being the one who started the fires. He did it. I might have been there and watched, but he made me go.'

'We do have evidence showing that you were the person who instigated it.'

'He's scared,' George said in her ear. 'His eyebrows are slightly raised, and his mouth half-open. You've got him.'

Whitney held out Jay's phone, displaying the messages. 'Shall I read them out to you?'

Mrs Hibbert leant in towards the phone and read them. 'Alfie. How could you?'

'They're not from my phone,' he said, his voice shaky.

'Give me your phone,' Whitney said.

'I don't have it with me,' he said.

'Yes, you do. You were on it a few moments ago,' his mother said, in a sharp voice. 'Give it to the officer.'

'It's in my pocket.'

'Take it out and give it to me. Open it first,' Mrs Hibbert said.

He unlocked the phone and gave it to his mother, who then passed it over to Whitney.

Whitney read the messages. 'This confirms that the texts on Jay's phone were from you.' She went into the photos app and clicked on videos. It was empty. 'Where's the video Jay took of you talking about what you'd done?'

'What video?' he said.

'I'm taking this phone in as evidence.' Even if he'd deleted it, Ellie would be able to find it.

'You can't take my phone.'

'Yes, I can.' She pulled out an evidence bag from her pocket and dropped his phone into it.

'I want to ask you again about Charlotte Payne. Did she ask

you to set the fire which caused the deaths of Hannah, Lucy, and Oscar Drinkwater?'

A sob escaped the lips of Mrs Hibbert, and Whitney passed over the box of tissues. 'Oh Alfie,' Mrs Hibbert said sniffing. 'Why? Those poor defenceless children. How could you?'

His face crumpled. Was he finally realising the consequences of what he'd done?

'I wanted to help her. She didn't ask me to do it, but she was so upset because Simon wouldn't leave the family. She—'

'Alfie Hibbert, I'm arresting you on suspicion of starting the fires in Stanton Road, Brook Street, Rushmere Close, and Wellington Street, and causing the deaths of twenty-seven people,' Whitney said, interrupting. 'You do not have to say anything, but it may harm your defence if you do not mention when questioned something which you later rely on in court. Anything you do say may be given in evidence. Do you understand?'

'Yes,' he said.

'What happens now?' Mrs Hibbert asked.

'Alfie will be formally charged and taken into custody until his bail hearing.'

'I'm going to say I couldn't help it. That there's something wrong with me that makes me do it. You'll have to take me to a psychiatrist or someone. They can show that I couldn't help it.'

If she had a pound for every time she was fed that line, she'd be very rich.

'Everything will happen in due course. You'll need a solicitor,' Whitney said, ignoring Alfie and focusing on Mrs Hibbert.

'I can't afford it. I've got no money. We live from week to week on my wages.'

'We can arrange for a duty solicitor to represent Alfie, after which time we will formally interview him again.'

'Can I be present?' Mrs Hibbert asked.

'Yes, you can be present at all times.' She turned to the boy.

'Alfie, Detective Sergeant Price will escort you to the custody suite.'

'What about me?' Mrs Hibbert said.

'You are welcome to stay, but we won't be interviewing Alfie again for some time. Maybe you should go home, and we'll be in touch.'

'Can I stay with him for now?'

'Yes. Until he's shown to his cell,' Whitney said.

Matt took the boy and his mother out and Whitney went to see George.

'It's finally over. But what a mess.'

'What about the other boy?'

'He'll be charged as an accessory, but I suspect he'll be looked on sympathetically. I've got to go and see Jamieson now. Want to go out for a drink after?'

'I've cancelled Ross, so I've got nothing else on.'

'Okay, wait for me in my office. I won't be too long.'

She headed upstairs to Jamieson's office.

'Sir, I've come to let you know, we've arrested two fifteen-year-old boys for the fires. One of them we'll be charging as an accessory, as he was there under duress.'

'Good work, Walker. I'm glad that you're here now because I've got some news for you.'

News? About the move? His job? Or her job?

She sucked in a breath. 'What is it?'

'I've been offered a position as Head of Intelligence Analysis for South Wales Police, and I'm seriously considering it.'

Whitney's head snapped up.

He was leaving?

'So, you don't want to stay here?'

'No, I don't think I do. Not with the way the new senior management team is shaping up. I'm trusting you not to say anything as nothing's confirmed yet and I haven't signed the contract.'

What did he know that he wasn't sharing?

'I'll keep it confidential, sir. Do you know yet when the rest of us will be hearing about our jobs?'

'At the start of next week, you'll find out about your future.'

THIRTY-FOUR

Monday, 28 September

George went to the bar and ordered a pint for herself and a wine for Whitney, while her friend went to the ladies. She took the drinks and a couple of menus to a table in the corner. After five minutes Whitney returned and made a beeline for the table.

Whitney sat opposite and took a sip of her wine. 'I needed that. We've solved the case, but I can't help feeling sorry for the parents of the boys. To find out what their kids had done, especially Mrs Hibbert. I doubt they'll ever get over it.'

'I'm assuming Alfie will be incarcerated, but what about Jay?'

'He acted under duress and I'm hoping that the judge will take that into consideration and he won't be locked up in a young offender institution. It would do more harm than good if he was.'

'I agree. Once away from Alfie's influence and with the stability of his home life, he should come through this.'

'I hope so.'

'Will there be any repercussions for the gang and Charlotte Payne?'

'The gang is now on our radar much more than previously, even though Alfie wasn't acting under their instruction. As for Charlotte Payne, her relationship with Simon Drinkwater is over, but that's it. She, too, had no idea what Alfie had done and can't be held to blame. All she ever did was moan about the family to the boy. He took matters into his own hands.'

'He may claim diminished responsibility, but from my observations I doubt that will stick. He knew exactly what he was doing,' George said.

'It drives me crazy the way offenders try that one on. But we'll have to wait and see.'

George handed her a menu. 'I assumed you'd want something to eat.'

'Thanks,' Whitney said, taking the menu from her and staring at it. 'I'll have scampi and chips, and no doubt you're going to have a salad.' She placed the menu on the table.

'Actually, I'm not,' George said. 'I fancy something a bit more substantial.'

When she came back from having ordered their food Whitney was sitting there with a smile on her face.

'You're looking very happy.'

'Of course I am. We've solved the case.'

'No, you're happier than you would be if it was just that. Something else has happened. Your eyes are gleaming.'

'I can't keep anything from you. You're right. I was remembering the conversation I had with Jamieson before we came out. He told me he's thinking about taking a job he's been offered in Wales. He's finally going.'

'That explains your uplifted mood.'

'It certainly does. I think we should drink to Jamieson's departure.'

'If that's what you'd like to do,' George said, holding up her glass.

'He did tell me not to mention it to anyone because it isn't official, as he hasn't signed the contract. You don't count as *anyone* because I know you're not going to tell.'

'You're right, I won't,' George said. 'Don't get too excited, though, as you know what happened the last time you thought he was on his way.'

'I'm going to ignore that. Here's to the end of the Jamieson and Walker era,' Whitney said, smiling, as she clinked her glass against George's.

'If Jamieson isn't here, there's bound to be someone else to annoy you, because that's what you're like.'

'That's unfair,' Whitney said, placing her glass on the table and glaring at her. 'I resent being categorised like that.'

Had she overstepped the mark? She didn't think so. If the roles were reversed Whitney would have had no qualms in saying what she thought.

'Throughout your working life, as you know, you haven't seen eye to eye with people. Especially those superior to you. There was—'

'Not everyone,' Whitney interrupted. 'Don Mason was the best boss ever, and we didn't fall out. Not ever ... well, there was the occasional time we didn't totally agree, but—'

'He was the exception to the rule,' George said.

'I only fall out with those who deserve it, like Dickhead Douglas. You've met him and know exactly what he's like so surely you're not counting him.'

'I didn't approve of the way he operated, and his treatment of you wasn't acceptable. In that instance I do agree.'

'It would be just my luck for him to be working at the new station, especially as he's now been promoted to chief superintendent.' She paused. 'Why the hell did you mention him, are you trying to spoil the evening for me?'

'You were the one who mentioned him by name after I'd passed comment on how you have issues with people in a higher position.'

'And, as I said, only those who I think are incompetent at their job. Whoever takes Jamieson's place I'll make an extra special effort to get on with them. Providing they're not—'

'Providing they're not what?' George said interrupting. 'On the fast-track scheme. Or providing they don't want things done their way and not yours?' She arched an eyebrow.

'Stop having a go at me.' Whitney's bottom lip stuck out until she realised what she was doing and forced it back in. Sounding like a petulant child wasn't cool.

'I'm making a point, that's all.'

'You can make whatever point you like. Jamieson's on his way and I'm happy about it. Bring on the next person, that's what I say. Now, tell me more about you and Ross. You've already said that you're seeing him again, but is it serious?'

'There's nothing else to add to our earlier conversations.'

'I think there is. You're not the only one who can recognise body language. I've been hanging around you long enough to work out when you're avoiding a discussion.'

'Touché. Okay, I'm prepared to give you an explanation. I've weighed everything up and, after seeing him several times since the exhibition, I realise that I do want our relationship to continue. I admit that my life is a lot better with him in it and I'm going to continue seeing him and let matters take their own course.'

'Hoo-bloody-ray. You've finally realised that what you did was ridiculous. Those months without him you weren't yourself. You weren't happy.'

'You may be right. I'm pleased that we're giving it another go.'

'So am I,' Whitney said, as she picked up her glass and took another drink.

Although her friend had much to be happy about, the tightness around her eyes was an indicator that the worry over her future still in the background.

'When will you be informed about the outcome of the restructure?'

'According to Jamieson I'll know next week. I've got a long few days ahead of me.'

'You do a good job and have a high clean-up rate for your cases. It would be ridiculous for you not to retain your position.'

'And here we have you jinxing yet again,' Whitney said, letting out an exasperated sigh.

'I've told you before about jinxing. It isn't a thing.' George shook her head in frustration. What was it with the woman that she placed so much importance on something with no scientific basis?

'Yes, it is. As we've proved time and time again. Thanks for that, George.'

'I refuse to be held responsible for whatever fate befalls you.'

'It's too late for that. You'd better hope my job is safe, or ...'

'Or?' George said, frowning.

'I'll be moving into your beautiful immaculate house and bringing my mess with me.'

'What?'

Whitney collapsed with laughter. 'Your face was a picture. You didn't think I was serious, did you?'

'I knew you were joking,' George lied.

'Of course, you did. Come on. Drink up. No more mention of what's going to happen to me. I just want to celebrate the solving of the case.'

A LETTER FROM THE AUTHOR

Dear reader,

Huge thanks for reading *Mortal Remains.* I hope you were hooked on the Cavendish and Walker series. If you want to join other readers in hearing all about my new releases and bonus content, you can sign up for my newsletter.

www.stormpublishing.co/sally-rigby

If you enjoyed this book and could spare a few moments to leave a review that would be hugely appreciated. Even a short review can make all the difference in encouraging a reader to discover my books for the first time. Thank you so much!

Thanks again for being part of this amazing journey with me and I hope you'll stay in touch—I have so many more stories and ideas to entertain you with!

Sally Rigby

www.sallyrigby.com

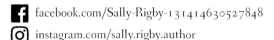

facebook.com/Sally-Rigby-131414630527848
instagram.com/sally.rigby.author

ACKNOWLEDGEMENTS

It's amazing that I've already reached book 8 in the series. I wouldn't have got this far without the help of my friends and critique partners, Amanda Ashby and Christina Phillips. Their support and friendship has been invaluable.

So many other people have helped bring this book to fruition. Emma Mitchell, my fantastic editor, who makes me dig deeper into the characters and the situations they find themselves in, thank you. I also couldn't have done this without the help of Kate Noble and my incredible advanced reader team. They pick up so much for me to work on.

I want to thank the genius, Stuart Bache, my cover designer. He never disappoints, and this cover just blew me away when he sent it.

To my family, Garry, Alicia and Marcus, and my parents Brenda and Geoffrey, I couldn't do this without your support. Thanks, also, to my brother Andrew for always reading and feeding back.

Printed in Great Britain
by Amazon